Idle Thoughts of an Idle Fellow

Idle Thoughts of an Idle Fellow

by Jerome K. Jerome

©2008 Wilder Publications

Wilder Publications, LLC.
PO Box 3005
Radford VA 24143-3005

ISBN 10: 1-60459-703-8
ISBN 13: 978-1-60459-703-5

Preface

One or two friends to whom I showed these papers in MS. having observed that they were not half bad, and some of my relations having promised to buy the book if it ever came out, I feel I have no right to longer delay its issue. But for this, as one may say, public demand, I perhaps should not have ventured to offer these mere "idle thoughts" of mine as mental food for the English-speaking peoples of the earth. What readers ask nowadays in a book is that it should improve, instruct, and elevate. This book wouldn't elevate a cow. I cannot conscientiously recommend it for any useful purposes whatever. All I can suggest is that when you get tired of reading "the best hundred books," you may take this up for half an hour. It will be a change.

On Being Idle.

Now, this is a subject on which I flatter myself I really am *au fait*. The gentleman who, when I was young, bathed me at wisdom's font for nine guineas a term—no extras—used to say he never knew a boy who could do less work in more time; and I remember my poor grandmother once incidentally observing, in the course of an instruction upon the use of the Prayer-book, that it was highly improbable that I should ever do much that I ought not to do, but that she felt convinced beyond a doubt that I should leave undone pretty well everything that I ought to do.

I am afraid I have somewhat belied half the dear old lady's prophecy. Heaven help me! I have done a good many things that I ought not to have done, in spite of my laziness. But I have fully confirmed the accuracy of her judgment so far as neglecting much that I ought not to have neglected is concerned. Idling always has been my strong point. I take no credit to myself in the matter—it is a gift. Few possess it. There are plenty of lazy people and plenty of slow-coaches, but a genuine idler is a rarity. He is not a man who slouches about with his hands in his pockets. On the contrary, his most startling characteristic is that he is always intensely busy.

It is impossible to enjoy idling thoroughly unless one has plenty of work to do. There is no fun in doing nothing when you have nothing to do. Wasting time is merely an occupation then, and a most exhausting one. Idleness, like kisses, to be sweet must be stolen.

Many years ago, when I was a young man, I was taken very ill—I never could see myself that much was the matter with me, except that I had a beastly cold. But I suppose it was something very serious, for the doctor said that I ought to have come to him a month before, and that if it (whatever it was) had gone on for another week he would not have answered for the consequences. It is an extraordinary thing, but I never knew a doctor called into any case yet but what it transpired that another day's delay would have rendered cure hopeless. Our medical guide, philosopher, and friend is like the hero in a melodrama—he always comes upon the scene just, and only just, in the nick of time. It is Providence, that is what it is.

Well, as I was saying, I was very ill and was ordered to Buxton for a month, with strict injunctions to do nothing whatever all the while that I was there. "Rest is what you require," said the doctor, "perfect rest."

It seemed a delightful prospect. "This man evidently understands my complaint," said I, and I pictured to myself a glorious time—a four weeks' *dolce far niente* with a dash of illness in it. Not too much illness, but just illness enough—just sufficient to give it the flavor of suffering and make it poetical. I should get up late, sip chocolate, and have my breakfast in slippers and a dressing-gown. I should lie out in the garden in a hammock and read sentimental novels with a melancholy ending, until the books should fall from my listless hand, and I should recline there, dreamily gazing into the deep blue of the firmament, watching the fleecy clouds floating like white-sailed ships across its depths, and listening to the joyous song of the birds and the low rustling of the trees. Or, on becoming too weak to go out of doors, I should sit propped up with pillows at the open window of the ground-floor front, and look wasted and interesting, so that all the pretty girls would sigh as they passed by.

And twice a day I should go down in a Bath chair to the Colonnade to drink the waters. Oh, those waters! I knew nothing about them then, and was rather taken with the idea. "Drinking the waters" sounded fashionable and Queen Anne-fied, and I thought I should like them. But, ugh! after the first three or four mornings! Sam Weller's description of them as "having a taste of warm flat-irons" conveys only a faint idea of their hideous nauseousness. If anything could make a sick man get well quickly, it would be the knowledge that he must drink a glassful of them every day until he was recovered. I drank them neat for six consecutive days, and they nearly killed me; but after then I adopted the plan of taking a stiff glass of brandy-and-water immediately on the top of them, and found much relief thereby. I have been informed since, by various eminent medical gentlemen, that the alcohol must have entirely counteracted the effects of the chalybeate properties contained in the water. I am glad I was lucky enough to hit upon the right thing.

But "drinking the waters" was only a small portion of the torture I experienced during that memorable month—a month which was, without exception, the most miserable I have ever spent. During the best part of it I religiously followed the doctor's mandate and did nothing whatever, except moon about the house and garden and go out for two hours a day in a Bath chair. That did break the monotony to a certain extent. There is more excitement about Bath-chairing—especially if you are not used to the exhilarating exercise—than might appear to the casual observer. A sense of danger, such as a mere outsider might not understand, is ever present to the mind of the occupant. He feels convinced every minute that the whole concern is going over, a conviction which becomes especially lively whenever a ditch or a stretch of newly macadamized road comes in sight. Every vehicle that passes he expects is going to run into him; and he never finds himself ascending or descending a hill without immediately beginning to speculate upon his chances, supposing—as seems extremely probable—that the weak-kneed controller of his destiny should let go.

But even this diversion failed to enliven after awhile, and the *ennui* became perfectly unbearable. I felt my mind giving way under it. It is not a strong mind, and I thought it would be unwise to tax it too far. So somewhere about the twentieth morning I got up early, had a good breakfast, and walked straight off to Hayfield, at the foot of the Kinder Scout—a pleasant, busy little town, reached through a lovely valley, and with two sweetly pretty women in it. At least they were sweetly pretty then; one passed me on the bridge and, I think, smiled; and the other was standing at an open door, making an unremunerative investment of kisses upon a red-faced baby. But it is years ago, and I dare say they have both grown stout and snappish since that time. Coming back, I saw an old man breaking stones, and it roused such strong longing in me to use my arms that I offered him a drink to let me take his place. He was a kindly old man and he humored me. I went for those stones with the accumulated energy of three weeks, and did more work in half an hour than he had done all day. But it did not make him jealous.

Having taken the plunge, I went further and further into dissipation, going out for a long walk every morning and listening to the band in the pavilion every evening. But the days still passed slowly notwithstanding, and I was heartily glad when the last one came and I was being whirled away from gouty, consumptive Buxton to London with its stern work and life. I looked out of the carriage as we rushed through Hendon in the evening. The lurid glare overhanging the mighty city seemed to warm my heart, and when, later on, my cab rattled out of St. Pancras' station, the old familiar roar that came swelling up around me sounded the sweetest music I had heard for many a long day.

I certainly did not enjoy that month's idling. I like idling when I ought not to be idling; not when it is the only thing I have to do. That is my pig-headed nature. The time when I like best to stand with my back to the fire, calculating how much I owe, is when my desk is heaped highest with letters that must be answered by the next post. When I like to dawdle longest over my dinner is when I have a heavy evening's work before me. And if, for some urgent reason, I ought to be up particularly early in the morning, it is then, more than at any other time, that I love to lie an extra half-hour in bed.

Ah! how delicious it is to turn over and go to sleep again: "just for five minutes." Is there any human being, I wonder, besides the hero of a Sunday-school "tale for boys," who ever gets up willingly? There are some men to whom getting up at the proper time is an utter impossibility. If eight o'clock happens to be the time that they should turn out, then they lie till half-past. If circumstances change and half-past eight becomes early enough for them, then it is nine before they can rise. They are like the statesman of whom it was said that he was always punctually half an hour late. They try all manner of schemes. They buy alarm-clocks (artful contrivances that go off at the wrong time and alarm the wrong people). They tell Sarah Jane to knock at the door and call them, and Sarah Jane does knock at the door and does call them, and they grunt back "awri" and then go comfortably to sleep again. I knew one man who would actually get out and have a cold bath; and even that was of no use, for afterward he would jump into bed again to warm himself.

I think myself that I could keep out of bed all right if I once got out. It is the wrenching away of the head from the pillow that I find so hard, and no amount of over-night determination makes it easier. I say to myself, after having wasted the whole evening, "Well, I won't do any more work to-night; I'll get up early to-morrow morning;" and I am thoroughly resolved to do so—then. In the morning, however, I feel less enthusiastic about the idea, and reflect that it would have been much better if I had stopped up last night. And then there is the trouble of dressing, and the more one thinks about that the more one wants to put it off.

It is a strange thing this bed, this mimic grave, where we stretch our tired limbs and sink away so quietly into the silence and rest. "O bed, O bed, delicious bed, that heaven on earth to the weary head," as sang poor Hood, you are a kind old nurse to us fretful boys and girls. Clever and foolish, naughty and good, you take us all in your motherly lap and hush our wayward crying. The strong man full of care—the sick man full of pain—the little maiden sobbing for her faithless lover—like children we lay our aching heads on your white bosom, and you gently soothe us off to by-by.

Our trouble is sore indeed when you turn away and will not comfort us. How long the dawn seems coming when we cannot sleep! Oh! those hideous nights when we toss and turn in fever and pain, when we lie, like living men among the dead, staring out into the dark hours that drift so slowly between us and the light. And oh! those still more hideous nights when we sit by another in pain, when the low fire startles us every now and then with a falling cinder, and the tick of the clock seems a hammer beating out the life that we are watching.

But enough of beds and bedrooms. I have kept to them too long, even for an idle fellow. Let us come out and have a smoke. That wastes time just as well and does not look so bad. Tobacco has been a blessing to us idlers. What the civil-service clerk before Sir Walter's time found to occupy their minds with it is hard to imagine. I attribute the quarrelsome nature of the Middle Ages young men entirely to the want of the soothing weed. They had no work to do and could not smoke, and the consequence was they were forever fighting and rowing. If, by any extraordinary chance, there was no war going, then they got up a deadly family feud with the next-door neighbor, and if, in spite of this, they still had a few spare moments on their hands, they occupied them with discussions as to whose sweetheart was the best looking, the arguments employed on both sides being battle-axes, clubs, etc. Questions of taste were soon decided in those days. When a twelfth-century youth fell in love he did not take three paces backward, gaze into her eyes, and tell her she was too beautiful to live. He said he would step outside and see about it. And if, when he got out, he met a man and broke his head—the other man's head, I mean—then that proved that his—the first fellow's—girl was a pretty girl. But if the other fellow broke *his* head—not his own, you know, but the other fellow's—the other fellow to the second fellow, that is, because of course the other fellow would only be the other fellow to him, not the first fellow who—well, if he broke his head, then *his* girl—not the other fellow's, but the fellow who *was* the—Look here, if A broke B's head, then A's girl was a pretty girl; but if B broke A's head, then A's girl wasn't a pretty girl, but B's girl was. That was their method of conducting art criticism.

Nowadays we light a pipe and let the girls fight it out among themselves.

They do it very well. They are getting to do all our work. They are doctors, and barristers, and artists. They manage theaters, and promote swindles, and edit newspapers. I am looking forward to the time when we men shall have nothing to do but lie in bed till twelve, read two novels a day, have nice little five-o'clock teas all to ourselves, and tax our brains with nothing more trying than discussions upon the latest patterns in trousers and arguments as to what Mr. Jones' coat was made of and whether it fitted him. It is a glorious prospect—for idle fellows.

On Being in Love.

You've been in love, of course! If not you've got it to come. Love is like the measles; we all have to go through it. Also like the measles, we take it only once. One never need be afraid of catching it a second time. The man who has had it can go into the most dangerous places and play the most foolhardy tricks with perfect safety. He can picnic in shady woods, ramble through leafy aisles, and linger on mossy seats to watch the sunset. He fears a quiet country-house no more than he would his own club. He can join a family party to go down the Rhine. He can, to see the last of a friend, venture into the very jaws of the marriage ceremony itself. He can keep his head through the whirl of a ravishing waltz, and rest afterward in a dark conservatory, catching nothing more lasting than a cold. He can brave a moonlight walk adown sweet-scented lanes or a twilight pull among the somber rushes. He can get over a stile without danger, scramble through a tangled hedge without being caught, come down a slippery path without falling. He can look into sunny eyes and not be dazzled. He listens to the siren voices, yet sails on with unveered helm. He clasps white hands in his, but no electric "Lulu"-like force holds him bound in their dainty pressure.

No, we never sicken with love twice. Cupid spends no second arrow on the same heart. Love's handmaids are our life-long friends. Respect, and admiration, and affection, our doors may always be left open for, but their great celestial master, in his royal progress, pays but one visit and departs. We like, we cherish, we are very, very fond of—but we never love again. A man's heart is a firework that once in its time flashes heavenward. Meteor-like, it blazes for a moment and lights with its glory the whole world beneath. Then the night of our sordid commonplace life closes in around it, and the burned-out case, falling back to earth, lies useless and uncared for, slowly smoldering into ashes. Once, breaking loose from our prison bonds, we dare, as mighty old Prometheus dared, to scale the Olympian mount and snatch from Phoebus' chariot the fire of the gods. Happy those who, hastening down again ere it dies out, can kindle their earthly altars at its flame. Love is too pure a light to burn long among the noisome gases that we breathe, but before it is choked out we may use it as a torch to ignite the cozy fire of affection.

And, after all, that warming glow is more suited to our cold little back parlor of a world than is the burning spirit love. Love should be the vestal fire of some mighty temple—some vast dim fane whose organ music is the rolling of the spheres. Affection will burn cheerily when the white flame of love is flickered out. Affection is a fire that can be fed from day to day and be piled up ever higher as the wintry years draw nigh. Old men and women can sit by it with their thin hands clasped, the little children can nestle down in front, the friend and neighbor has his welcome corner by its side, and even shaggy Fido and sleek Titty can toast their noses at the bars.

Let us heap the coals of kindness upon that fire. Throw on your pleasant words, your gentle pressures of the hand, your thoughtful and unselfish deeds. Fan it with good-humor, patience, and forbearance. You can let the wind blow and the rain fall unheeded then, for your hearth will be warm and bright, and the faces round it will make sunshine in spite of the clouds without.

I am afraid, dear Edwin and Angelina, you expect too much from love. You think there is enough of your little hearts to feed this fierce, devouring passion for all your long lives. Ah, young folk! don't rely too much upon that unsteady flicker. It will dwindle and dwindle as the months roll on, and there is no replenishing the fuel. You will watch it die out in anger and disappointment. To each it will seem that it is the other who is growing colder. Edwin sees with bitterness that Angelina no longer runs to the gate to meet him, all smiles and blushes; and when he has a cough now she doesn't begin to cry and, putting her arms round his neck, say that she cannot live without him. The most she will probably do is to suggest a lozenge, and even that in a tone implying that it is the noise more than anything else she is anxious to get rid of.

Poor little Angelina, too, sheds silent tears, for Edwin has given up carrying her old handkerchief in the inside pocket of his waistcoat.

Both are astonished at the falling off in the other one, but neither sees their own change. If they did they would not suffer as they do. They would look for the cause in the right quarter—in the littleness of poor human nature—join hands over their common failing, and start building their house anew on a more earthly and enduring foundation. But we are so blind to our own shortcomings, so wide awake to those of others. Everything that happens to us is always the other person's fault. Angelina would have gone on loving Edwin forever and ever and ever if only Edwin had not grown so strange and different. Edwin would have adored Angelina through eternity if Angelina had only remained the same as when he first adored her.

It is a cheerless hour for you both when the lamp of love has gone out and the fire of affection is not yet lit, and you have to grope about in the cold, raw dawn of life to kindle it. God grant it catches light before the day is too far spent. Many sit shivering by the dead coals till night come.

But, there, of what use is it to preach? Who that feels the rush of young love through his veins can think it will ever flow feeble and slow! To the boy of twenty it seems impossible that he will not love as wildly at sixty as he does then. He cannot call to mind any middle-aged or elderly gentleman of his acquaintance who is known to exhibit symptoms of frantic attachment, but that does not interfere in his belief in himself. His love will never fall, whoever else's may. Nobody ever loved as he loves, and so, of course, the rest of the world's experience can be no guide in his case. Alas! alas! ere thirty he has joined the ranks of the sneerers. It is not his fault. Our passions, both the good and bad, cease with our blushes. We do not hate, nor grieve, nor joy, nor despair in our thirties like we did in our teens. Disappointment does not suggest suicide, and we quaff success without intoxication.

We take all things in a minor key as we grow older. There are few majestic passages in the later acts of life's opera. Ambition takes a less ambitious aim. Honor becomes more reasonable and conveniently adapts itself to circumstances. And love—love dies. "Irreverence for the dreams of youth" soon creeps like a killing frost upon our hearts. The tender shoots and the expanding flowers are nipped and withered, and of a vine that yearned to stretch its tendrils round the world there is left but a sapless stump.

My fair friends will deem all this rank heresy, I know. So far from a man's not loving after he has passed boyhood, it is not till there is a good deal of gray in his hair that they think his protestations at all worthy of attention. Young ladies take their notions of our sex from the novels written by their own, and compared with the monstrosities that masquerade for men in the pages of that nightmare literature, Pythagoras' plucked bird and Frankenstein's demon were fair average specimens of humanity.

In these so-called books, the chief lover, or Greek god, as he is admiringly referred to—by the way, they do not say which "Greek god" it is that the gentleman bears such a striking likeness to; it might be hump-backed Vulcan, or double-faced Janus, or even driveling Silenus, the god of abstruse mysteries. He resembles the whole family of them, however, in being a blackguard, and perhaps this is what is meant. To even the little manliness his classical prototypes possessed, though, he can lay no claim whatever, being a listless effeminate noodle, on the shady side of forty. But oh! the depth and strength of this elderly party's emotion for some bread-and-butter school-girl! Hide your heads, ye young Romeos and Leanders! this *blase* old beau loves with an hysterical fervor that requires four adjectives to every noun to properly describe.

It is well, dear ladies, for us old sinners that you study only books. Did you read mankind, you would know that the lad's shy stammering tells a truer tale than our bold eloquence. A boy's love comes from a full heart; a man's is more often the result of a full stomach. Indeed, a man's sluggish current may not be called love, compared with the rushing fountain that wells up when a boy's heart is struck with the heavenly rod. If you would taste love, drink of the pure stream that youth pours out at your feet. Do not wait till it has become a muddy river before you stoop to catch its waves.

Or is it that you like its bitter flavor—that the clear, limpid water is insipid to your palate and that the pollution of its after-course gives it a relish to your lips? Must we believe those who tell us that a hand foul with the filth of a shameful life is the only one a young girl cares to be caressed by?

That is the teaching that is bawled out day by day from between those yellow covers. Do they ever pause to think, I wonder, those devil's ladyhelps, what mischief they are doing crawling about God's garden, and telling childish Eves and silly Adams that sin is sweet and that decency is ridiculous and vulgar? How many an innocent girl do they not degrade into an evil-minded woman? To how many a weak lad do they not point out the dirty by-path as the shortest cut to a maiden's heart? It is not as if they wrote of life as it really is. Speak truth, and right will take care of itself. But their pictures are coarse daubs painted from the sickly fancies of their own diseased imagination.

We want to think of women not—as their own sex would show them—as Lorleis luring us to destruction, but as good angels beckoning us upward. They have more power for good or evil than they dream of. It is just at the very age when a man's character is forming that he tumbles into love, and then the lass he loves has the making or marring of him. Unconsciously he molds himself to what she would have him, good or bad. I am sorry to have to be ungallant enough to say that I do not think they always use their influence for the best. Too often the female world is bounded hard and fast within the limits of the commonplace. Their ideal hero is a prince of littleness, and to become that many a powerful mind, enchanted by love, is "lost to life and use and name and fame."

And yet, women, you could make us so much better if you only would. It rests with you, more than with all the preachers, to roll this world a little nearer heaven. Chivalry is not dead: it only sleeps for want of work to do. It is you who must wake it to noble deeds. You must be worthy of knightly worship.

You must be higher than ourselves. It was for Una that the Red Cross Knight did war. For no painted, mincing court dame could the dragon have been slain. Oh, ladies fair, be fair in mind and soul as well as face, so that brave knights may win glory in your service! Oh, woman, throw off your disguising cloaks of selfishness, effrontery, and affectation! Stand forth once more a queen in your royal robe of simple purity. A thousand swords, now rusting in ignoble sloth, shall leap from their scabbards to do battle for your honor against wrong. A thousand Sir Rolands shall lay lance in rest, and Fear, Avarice, Pleasure, and Ambition shall go down in the dust before your colors.

What noble deeds were we not ripe for in the days when we loved? What noble lives could we not have lived for her sake? Our love was a religion we could have died for. It was no mere human creature like ourselves that we adored. It was a queen that we paid homage to, a goddess that we worshiped.

And how madly we did worship! And how sweet it was to worship! Ah, lad, cherish love's young dream while it lasts! You will know too soon how truly little Tom Moore sang when he said that there was nothing half so sweet in life. Even when it brings misery it is a wild, romantic misery, all unlike the dull, worldly pain of after-sorrows. When you have lost her—when the light is gone out from your life and the world stretches before you a long, dark horror, even then a half-enchantment mingles with your despair.

And who would not risk its terrors to gain its raptures? Ah, what raptures they were! The mere recollection thrills you. How delicious it was to tell her that you loved her, that you lived for her, that you would die for her! How you did rave, to be sure, what floods of extravagant nonsense you poured forth, and oh, how cruel it was of her to pretend not to believe you! In what awe you stood of her! How miserable you were when you had offended her! And yet, how pleasant to be bullied by her and to sue for pardon without having the slightest notion of what your fault was! How dark the world was when she snubbed you, as she often did, the little rogue, just to see you look wretched; how sunny when she smiled! How jealous you were of every one about her! How you hated every man she shook hands with, every woman she kissed—the maid that did her hair, the boy that cleaned her shoes, the dog she nursed—though you had to be respectful to the last-named! How you looked forward to seeing her, how stupid you were when you did see her, staring at her without saying a word! How impossible it was for you to go out at any time of the day or night without finding yourself eventually opposite her windows! You hadn't pluck enough to go in, but you hung about the corner and gazed at the outside. Oh, if the house had only caught fire—it was insured, so it wouldn't have mattered—and you could have rushed in and saved her at the risk of your life, and have been terribly burned and injured! Anything to serve her. Even in little things that was so sweet. How you would watch her, spaniel-like, to anticipate her slightest wish! How proud you were to do her bidding! How delightful it was to be ordered about by her! To devote your whole life to her and to never think of yourself seemed such a simple thing. You would go without a holiday to lay a humble offering at her shrine, and felt more than repaid if she only deigned to accept it. How precious to you was everything that she had hallowed by her touch—her little glove, the ribbon she had worn, the rose that had nestled in her hair and whose withered leaves still mark the poems you never care to look at now.

And oh, how beautiful she was, how wondrous beautiful! It was as some angel entering the room, and all else became plain and earthly. She was too sacred to be touched. It seemed almost presumption to gaze at her. You would as soon have thought of kissing her as of singing comic songs in a cathedral. It was desecration enough to kneel and timidly raise the gracious little hand to your lips.

Ah, those foolish days, those foolish days when we were unselfish and pure-minded; those foolish days when our simple hearts were full of truth, and faith, and reverence! Ah, those foolish days of noble longings and of noble strivings! And oh, these wise, clever days when we know that money is the only prize worth striving for, when we believe in nothing else but meanness and lies, when we care for no living creature but ourselves!

On Being in the Blues.

I can enjoy feeling melancholy, and there is a good deal of satisfaction about being thoroughly miserable; but nobody likes a fit of the blues. Nevertheless, everybody has them; notwithstanding which, nobody can tell why. There is no accounting for them. You are just as likely to have one on the day after you have come into a large fortune as on the day after you have left your new silk umbrella in the train. Its effect upon you is somewhat similar to what would probably be produced by a combined attack of toothache, indigestion, and cold in the head. You become stupid, restless, and irritable; rude to strangers and dangerous toward your friends; clumsy, maudlin, and quarrelsome; a nuisance to yourself and everybody about you.

While it is on you can do nothing and think of nothing, though feeling at the time bound to do something. You can't sit still so put on your hat and go for a walk; but before you get to the corner of the street you wish you hadn't come out and you turn back. You open a book and try to read, but you find Shakespeare trite and commonplace, Dickens is dull and prosy, Thackeray a bore, and Carlyle too sentimental. You throw the book aside and call the author names. Then you "shoo" the cat out of the room and kick the door to after her. You think you will write your letters, but after sticking at "Dearest Auntie: I find I have five minutes to spare, and so hasten to write to you," for a quarter of an hour, without being able to think of another sentence, you tumble the paper into the desk, fling the wet pen down upon the table-cloth, and start up with the resolution of going to see the Thompsons. While pulling on your gloves, however, it occurs to you that the Thompsons are idiots; that they never have supper; and that you will be expected to jump the baby. You curse the Thompsons and decide not to go.

By this time you feel completely crushed. You bury your face in your hands and think you would like to die and go to heaven. You picture to yourself your own sick-bed, with all your friends and relations standing round you weeping. You bless them all, especially the young and pretty ones. They will value you when you are gone, so you say to yourself, and learn too late what they have lost; and you bitterly contrast their presumed regard for you then with their decided want of veneration now.

These reflections make you feel a little more cheerful, but only for a brief period; for the next moment you think what a fool you must be to imagine for an instant that anybody would be sorry at anything that might happen to you. Who would care two straws (whatever precise amount of care two straws may represent) whether you are blown up, or hung up, or married, or drowned? Nobody cares for you. You never have been properly appreciated, never met with your due deserts in any one particular. You review the whole of your past life, and it is painfully apparent that you have been ill-used from your cradle.

Half an hour's indulgence in these considerations works you up into a state of savage fury against everybody and everything, especially yourself, whom anatomical reasons alone prevent your kicking. Bed-time at last comes, to save you from doing something rash, and you spring upstairs, throw off your clothes, leaving them strewn all over the room, blow out the candle, and jump into bed as if you had backed yourself for a heavy wager to do the whole thing against time. There you toss and tumble about for a couple of hours or so, varying the monotony by occasionally jerking the clothes off and getting out and putting them on again. At length you drop into an uneasy and fitful slumber, have bad dreams, and wake up late the next morning.

At least, this is all we poor single men can do under the circumstances. Married men bully their wives, grumble at the dinner, and insist on the children's going to bed. All of which, creating, as it does, a good deal of disturbance in the house, must be a great relief to the feelings of a man in the blues, rows being the only form of amusement in which he can take any interest.

The symptoms of the infirmity are much the same in every case, but the affliction itself is variously termed. The poet says that "a feeling of sadness comes o'er him." 'Arry refers to the heavings of his wayward heart by confiding to Jimee that he has "got the blooming hump." Your sister doesn't know what is the matter with her to-night. She feels out of sorts altogether and hopes nothing is going to happen. The every-day young man is "so awful glad to meet you, old fellow," for he does "feel so jolly miserable this evening." As for myself, I generally say that "I have a strange, unsettled feeling to-night" and "think I'll go out."

By the way, it never does come except in the evening. In the sun-time, when the world is bounding forward full of life, we cannot stay to sigh and sulk. The roar of the working day drowns the voices of the elfin sprites that are ever singing their low-toned *miserere* in our ears. In the day we are angry, disappointed, or indignant, but never "in the blues" and never melancholy. When things go wrong at ten o'clock in the morning we—or rather you—swear and knock the furniture about; but if the misfortune comes at ten P.M., we read poetry or sit in the dark and think what a hollow world this is.

But, as a rule, it is not trouble that makes us melancholy. The actuality is too stern a thing for sentiment. We linger to weep over a picture, but from the original we should quickly turn our eyes away. There is no pathos in real misery: no luxury in real grief. We do not toy with sharp swords nor hug a gnawing fox to our breast for choice. When a man or woman loves to brood over a sorrow and takes care to keep it green in their memory, you may be sure it is no longer a pain to them. However they may have suffered from it at first, the recollection has become by then a pleasure. Many dear old ladies who daily look at tiny shoes lying in lavender-scented drawers, and weep as they think of the tiny feet whose toddling march is done, and sweet-faced young ones who place each night beneath their pillow some lock that once curled on a boyish head that the salt waves have kissed to death, will call me a nasty cynical brute and say I'm talking nonsense; but I believe, nevertheless, that if they will ask themselves truthfully whether they find it unpleasant to dwell thus on their sorrow, they will be compelled to answer "No." Tears are as sweet as laughter to some natures. The proverbial Englishman, we know from old chronicler Froissart, takes his pleasures sadly, and the Englishwoman goes a step further and takes her pleasures in sadness itself.

I am not sneering. I would not for a moment sneer at anything that helps to keep hearts tender in this hard old world. We men are cold and common-sensed enough for all; we would not have women the same. No, no, ladies dear, be always sentimental and soft-hearted, as you are—be the soothing butter to our coarse dry bread. Besides, sentiment is to women what fun is to us. They do not care for our humor, surely it would be unfair to deny them their grief. And who shall say that their mode of enjoyment is not as sensible as ours? Why assume that a doubled-up body, a contorted, purple face, and a gaping mouth emitting a series of ear-splitting shrieks point to a state of more intelligent happiness than a pensive face reposing upon a little white hand, and a pair of gentle tear-dimmed eyes looking back through Time's dark avenue upon a fading past?

I am glad when I see Regret walked with as a friend—glad because I know the saltness has been washed from out the tears, and that the sting must have been plucked from the beautiful face of Sorrow ere we dare press her pale lips to ours. Time has laid his healing hand upon the wound when we can look back upon the pain we once fainted under and no bitterness or despair rises in our hearts. The burden is no longer heavy when we have for our past troubles only the same sweet mingling of pleasure and pity that we feel when old knight-hearted Colonel Newcome answers "*adsum*" to the great roll-call, or when Tom and Maggie Tulliver, clasping hands through the mists that have divided them, go down, locked in each other's arms, beneath the swollen waters of the Floss.

Talking of poor Tom and Maggie Tulliver brings to my mind a saying of George Eliot's in connection with this subject of melancholy. She speaks somewhere of the "sadness of a summer's evening." How wonderfully true—like everything that came from that wonderful pen—the observation is! Who has not felt the sorrowful enchantment of those lingering sunsets? The world belongs to Melancholy then, a thoughtful deep-eyed maiden who loves not the glare of day. It is not till "light thickens and the crow wings to the rocky wood" that she steals forth from her groves. Her palace is in twilight land. It is there she meets us. At her shadowy gate she takes our hand in hers and walks beside us through her mystic realm. We see no form, but seem to hear the rustling of her wings.

Even in the toiling hum-drum city her spirit comes to us. There is a somber presence in each long, dull street; and the dark river creeps ghostlike under the black arches, as if bearing some hidden secret beneath its muddy waves.

In the silent country, when the trees and hedges loom dim and blurred against the rising night, and the bat's wing flutters in our face, and the land-rail's cry sounds drearily across the fields, the spell sinks deeper still into our hearts. We seem in that hour to be standing by some unseen death-bed, and in the swaying of the elms we hear the sigh of the dying day.

A solemn sadness reigns. A great peace is around us. In its light our cares of the working day grow small and trivial, and bread and cheese—ay, and even kisses—do not seem the only things worth striving for. Thoughts we cannot speak but only listen to flood in upon us, and standing in the stillness under earth's darkening dome, we feel that we are greater than our petty lives. Hung round with those dusky curtains, the world is no longer a mere dingy workshop, but a stately temple wherein man may worship, and where at times in the dimness his groping hands touch God's.

On Being Hard Up.

It is a most remarkable thing. I sat down with the full intention of writing something clever and original; but for the life of me I can't think of anything clever and original—at least, not at this moment. The only thing I can think about now is being hard up. I suppose having my hands in my pockets has made me think about this. I always do sit with my hands in my pockets except when I am in the company of my sisters, my cousins, or my aunts; and they kick up such a shindy—I should say expostulate so eloquently upon the subject—that I have to give in and take them out—my hands I mean. The chorus to their objections is that it is not gentlemanly. I am hanged if I can see why. I could understand its not being considered gentlemanly to put your hands in other people's pockets (especially by the other people), but how, O ye sticklers for what looks this and what looks that, can putting his hands in his own pockets make a man less gentle? Perhaps you are right, though. Now I come to think of it, I have heard some people grumble most savagely when doing it. But they were mostly old gentlemen. We young fellows, as a rule, are never quite at ease unless we have our hands in our pockets. We are awkward and shifty. We are like what a music-hall Lion Comique would be without his opera-hat, if such a thing can be imagined. But let us put our hands in our trousers pockets, and let there be some small change in the right-hand one and a bunch of keys in the left, and we will face a female post-office clerk.

It is a little difficult to know what to do with your bands, even in your pockets, when there is nothing else there. Years ago, when my whole capital would occasionally come down to "what in town the people call a bob," I would recklessly spend a penny of it, merely for the sake of having the change, all in coppers, to jingle. You don't feel nearly so hard up with eleven pence in your pocket as you do with a shilling. Had I been "La-di-da," that impecunious youth about whom we superior folk are so sarcastic, I would have changed my penny for two ha'pennies.

I can speak with authority on the subject of being hard up. I have been a provincial actor. If further evidence be required, which I do not think likely, I can add that I have been a "gentleman connected with the press." I have lived on 15 shilling a week. I have lived a week on 10, owing the other 5; and I have lived for a fortnight on a great-coat.

It is wonderful what an insight into domestic economy being really hard up gives one. If you want to find out the value of money, live on 15 shillings a week and see how much you can put by for clothes and recreation. You will find out that it is worth while to wait for the farthing change, that it is worth while to walk a mile to save a penny, that a glass of beer is a luxury to be indulged in only at rare intervals, and that a collar can be worn for four days.

Try it just before you get married. It will be excellent practice. Let your son and heir try it before sending him to college. He won't grumble at a hundred a year pocket-money then. There are some people to whom it would do a world of good. There is that delicate blossom who can't drink any claret under ninety-four, and who would as soon think of dining off cat's meat as off plain roast mutton. You do come across these poor wretches now and then, though, to the credit of humanity, they are principally confined to that fearful and wonderful society known only to lady novelists. I never hear of one of these creatures discussing a *menu* card but I feel a mad desire to drag him off to the bar of some common east-end public-house and cram a sixpenny dinner down his throat—beefsteak pudding, fourpence; potatoes, a penny; half a pint of porter, a penny. The recollection of it (and the mingled fragrance of beer, tobacco, and roast pork generally leaves a vivid impression) might induce him to turn up his nose a little less frequently in the future at everything that is put before him. Then there is that generous party, the cadger's delight, who is so free with his small change, but who never thinks of paying his debts. It might teach even him a little common sense. "I always give the waiter a shilling. One can't give the fellow less, you know," explained a young government clerk with whom I was lunching the other day in Regent Street. I agreed with him as to the utter impossibility of making it elevenpence ha'penny; but at the same time I resolved to one day decoy him to an eating-house I remembered near Covent Garden, where the waiter, for the better discharge of his duties, goes about in his shirt-sleeves—and very dirty sleeves they are, too, when it gets near the end of the month. I know that waiter. If my friend gives him anything beyond a penny, the man will insist on shaking hands with him then and there as a mark of his esteem; of that I feel sure.

There have been a good many funny things said and written about hardupishness, but the reality is not funny, for all that. It is not funny to have to haggle over pennies. It isn't funny to be thought mean and stingy. It isn't funny to be shabby and to be ashamed of your address. No, there is nothing at all funny in poverty—to the poor. It is hell upon earth to a sensitive man; and many a brave gentleman who would have faced the labors of Hercules has had his heart broken by its petty miseries.

It is not the actual discomforts themselves that are hard to bear. Who would mind roughing it a bit if that were all it meant? What cared Robinson

Crusoe for a patch on his trousers? Did he wear trousers? I forget; or did he go about as he does in the pantomimes? What did it matter to him if his toes did stick out of his boots? and what if his umbrella was a cotton one, so long as it kept the rain off? His shabbiness did not trouble him; there was none of his friends round about to sneer him.

Being poor is a mere trifle. It is being known to be poor that is the sting. It is not cold that makes a man without a great-coat hurry along so quickly. It is not all shame at telling lies—which he knows will not be believed—that makes him turn so red when he informs you that he considers great-coats unhealthy and never carries an umbrella on principle. It is easy enough to say that poverty is no crime. No; if it were men wouldn't be ashamed of it. It's a blunder, though, and is punished as such. A poor man is despised the whole world over; despised as much by a Christian as by a lord, as much by a demagogue as by a footman, and not all the copy-book maxims ever set for ink stained youth will make him respected. Appearances are everything, so far as human opinion goes, and the man who will walk down Piccadilly arm in arm with the most notorious scamp in London, provided he is a well-dressed one, will slink up a back street to say a couple of words to a seedy-looking gentleman. And the seedy-looking gentleman knows this—no one better—and will go a mile round to avoid meeting an acquaintance. Those that knew him in his prosperity need never trouble themselves to look the other way. He is a thousand times more anxious that they should not see him than they can be; and as to their assistance, there is nothing he dreads more than the offer of it. All he wants is to be forgotten; and in this respect he is generally fortunate enough to get what he wants.

One becomes used to being hard up, as one becomes used to everything else, by the help of that wonderful old homeopathic doctor, Time. You can tell at a glance the difference between the old hand and the novice; between the case-hardened man who has been used to shift and struggle for years and the poor devil of a beginner striving to hide his misery, and in a constant agony of fear lest he should be found out. Nothing shows this difference more clearly than the way in which each will pawn his watch. As the poet says somewhere: "True ease in pawning comes from art, not chance." The one goes into his "uncle's" with as much composure as he would into his tailor's—very likely with more. The assistant is even civil and attends to him at once, to the great indignation of the lady in the next box, who, however, sarcastically observes that she don't mind being kept waiting "if it is a regular customer." Why, from the pleasant and businesslike manner in which the transaction is carried out, it might be a large purchase in the three per cents. Yet what a piece of work a man makes of his first "pop." A boy popping his first question is confidence itself compared with him. He hangs about outside the shop until he has succeeded in attracting the attention of all the loafers in the neighborhood and has aroused strong suspicions in the mind of the policeman on the beat. At last, after a careful examination of the contents of the windows, made for the purpose of impressing the bystanders with the notion that he is going in to purchase a diamond bracelet or some such trifle, he enters, trying to do so with a careless swagger, and giving himself really the air of a member of the swell mob. When inside he speaks in so low a voice as to be perfectly inaudible, and has to say it all over again. When, in the course of his rambling conversation about a "friend" of his, the word "lend" is reached, he is promptly told to go up the court on the right and take the first door round the corner. He comes out of the shop with a face that you could easily light a cigarette at, and firmly under the impression that the whole population of the district is watching him. When he does get to the right place he has forgotten his name and address and is in a general condition of hopeless imbecility. Asked in a severe tone how he came by "this," he stammers and contradicts himself, and it is only a miracle if he does not confess to having stolen it that very day. He is thereupon informed that they don't want anything to do with his sort, and that he had better get out of this as quickly as possible, which he does, recollecting nothing more until he finds himself three miles off, without the slightest knowledge how he got there.

By the way, how awkward it is, though, having to depend on public-houses and churches for the time. The former are generally too fast and the latter too slow. Besides which, your efforts to get a glimpse of the public house clock from the outside are attended with great difficulties. If you gently push the swing-door ajar and peer in you draw upon yourself the contemptuous looks of the barmaid, who at once puts you down in the same category with area sneaks and cadgers. You also create a certain amount of agitation among the married portion of the customers. You don't see the clock because it is behind the door; and in trying to withdraw quietly you jam your head. The only other method is to jump up and down outside the window. After this latter proceeding, however, if you do not bring out a banjo and commence to sing, the youthful inhabitants of the neighborhood, who have gathered round in expectation, become disappointed.

I should like to know, too, by what mysterious law of nature it is that before you have left your watch "to be repaired" half an hour, some one is sure to stop you in the street and conspicuously ask you the time. Nobody even feels the slightest curiosity on the subject when you've got it on.

Dear old ladies and gentlemen who know nothing about being hard up—and may they never, bless their gray old heads—look upon the pawn-shop as the last stage of degradation; but those who know it better (and my readers have no doubt, noticed this themselves) are often surprised, like the little boy who dreamed he went to heaven, at meeting so many people there that they never expected to see. For my part, I think it a much more independent course than borrowing from friends, and I always try to impress this upon those of my acquaintance who incline toward "wanting a couple of pounds till the day after to-morrow." But they won't all see it. One of them once remarked that he objected to the principle of the thing. I fancy if he had said it was the interest that he objected to he would have been nearer the truth: twenty-five per cent. certainly does come heavy.

There are degrees in being hard up. We are all hard up, more or less—most of us more. Some are hard up for a thousand pounds; some for a shilling. Just at this moment I am hard up myself for a fiver. I only want it for a day or two. I should be certain of paying it back within a week at the outside, and if any lady or gentleman among my readers would kindly lend it me, I should be very much obliged indeed. They could send it to me under cover to Messrs. Field & Tuer, only, in such case, please let the envelope be carefully sealed. I would give you my I.O.U. as security.

On Vanity and Vanities.

All is vanity and everybody's vain. Women are terribly vain. So are men—more so, if possible. So are children, particularly children. One of them at this very moment is hammering upon my legs. She wants to know what I think of her new shoes. Candidly I don't think much of them. They lack symmetry and curve and possess an indescribable appearance of lumpiness (I believe, too, they've put them on the wrong feet). But I don't say this. It is not criticism, but flattery that she wants; and I gush over them with what I feel to myself to be degrading effusiveness. Nothing else would satisfy this self-opinionated cherub. I tried the conscientious-friend dodge with her on one occasion, but it was not a success. She had requested my judgment upon her general conduct and behavior, the exact case submitted being, "Wot oo tink of me? Oo peased wi' me?" and I had thought it a good opportunity to make a few salutary remarks upon her late moral career, and said: "No, I am not pleased with you." I recalled to her mind the events of that very morning, and I put it to her how she, as a Christian child, could expect a wise and good uncle to be satisfied with the carryings on of an infant who that very day had roused the whole house at five AM.; had upset a water-jug and tumbled downstairs after it at seven; had endeavored to put the cat in the bath at eight; and sat on her own father's hat at nine thirty-five.

What did she do? Was she grateful to me for my plain speaking? Did she ponder upon my words and determine to profit by them and to lead from that hour a better and nobler life?

No! she howled.

That done, she became abusive. She said:

"Oo naughty—oo naughty, bad unkie—oo bad man—me tell MAR."

And she did, too.

Since then, when my views have been called for I have kept my real sentiments more to myself like, preferring to express unbounded admiration of this young person's actions, irrespective of their actual merits. And she nods her head approvingly and trots off to advertise my opinion to the rest of the household. She appears to employ it as a sort of testimonial for mercenary purposes, for I subsequently hear distant sounds of "Unkie says me dood dirl—me dot to have two bikkies [biscuits]."

There she goes, now, gazing rapturously at her own toes and murmuring "pittie"—two-foot-ten of conceit and vanity, to say nothing of other wickednesses.

They are all alike. I remember sitting in a garden one sunny afternoon in the suburbs of London. Suddenly I heard a shrill treble voice calling from a top-story window to some unseen being, presumably in one of the other gardens, "Gamma, me dood boy, me wery good boy, gamma; me dot on Bob's knickiebockies."

Why, even animals are vain. I saw a great Newfoundland dog the other day sitting in front of a mirror at the entrance to a shop in Regent's Circus, and examining himself with an amount of smug satisfaction that I have never seen equaled elsewhere outside a vestry meeting.

I was at a farm-house once when some high holiday was being celebrated. I don't remember what the occasion was, but it was something festive, a May Day or Quarter Day, or something of that sort, and they put a garland of flowers round the head of one of the cows. Well, that absurd quadruped went about all day as perky as a schoolgirl in a new frock; and when they took the wreath off she became quite sulky, and they had to put it on again before she would stand still to be milked. This is not a Percy anecdote. It is plain, sober truth.

As for cats, they nearly equal human beings for vanity. I have known a cat get up and walk out of the room on a remark derogatory to her species being made by a visitor, while a neatly turned compliment will set them purring for an hour.

I do like cats. They are so unconsciously amusing. There is such a comic dignity about them, such a "How dare you!" "Go away, don't touch me" sort of air. Now, there is nothing haughty about a dog. They are "Hail, fellow, well met" with every Tom, Dick, or Harry that they come across. When I meet a dog of my acquaintance I slap his head, call him opprobrious epithets, and roll him over on his back; and there he lies, gaping at me, and doesn't mind it a bit.

Fancy carrying on like that with a cat! Why, she would never speak to you again as long as you lived. No, when you want to win the approbation of a cat you must mind what you are about and work your way carefully. If you don't know the cat, you had best begin by saying, "Poor pussy." After which add "did 'ums" in a tone of soothing sympathy. You don't know what you mean any more than the cat does, but the sentiment seems to imply a proper spirit on your part, and generally touches her feelings to such an extent that if you are of good manners and passable appearance she will stick her back up and rub her nose against you. Matters having reached this stage, you may venture to chuck her under the chin and tickle the side of her head, and the intelligent creature will then stick her claws into your legs; and all is friendship and affection, as so sweetly expressed in the beautiful lines—

> "I love little pussy, her coat is so warm,
> And if I don't tease her she'll do me no harm;
> So I'll stroke her, and pat her, and feed her with food,
> And pussy will love me because I am good."

The last two lines of the stanza give us a pretty true insight into pussy's notions of human goodness. It is evident that in her opinion goodness consists of stroking her, and patting her, and feeding her with food. I fear this narrow-minded view of virtue, though, is not confined to pussies. We are all inclined to adopt a similar standard of merit in our estimate of other people. A good man is a man who is good to us, and a bad man is a man who doesn't do what we want him to. The truth is, we each of us have an inborn conviction that the whole world, with everybody and everything in it, was created as a sort of necessary appendage to ourselves. Our fellow men and women were made to admire us and to minister to our various requirements. You and I, dear reader, are each the center of the universe in our respective opinions. You, as I understand it, were brought into being by a considerate Providence in order that you might read and pay me for what I write; while I, in your opinion, am an article sent into the world to write something for you to read. The stars—as we term the myriad other worlds that are rushing down beside us through the eternal silence—were put into the heavens to make the sky look interesting for us at night; and the moon with its dark mysteries and ever-hidden face is an arrangement for us to flirt under.

I fear we are most of us like Mrs. Poyser's bantam cock, who fancied the sun got up every morning to hear him crow. "'Tis vanity that makes the world go round." I don't believe any man ever existed without vanity, and if he did he would be an extremely uncomfortable person to have anything to do with. He would, of course, be a very good man, and we should respect him very much. He would be a very admirable man—a man to be put under a glass case and shown round as a specimen—a man to be stuck upon a pedestal and copied, like a school exercise—a man to be reverenced, but not a man to be loved, not a human brother whose hand we should care to grip. Angels may be very excellent sort of folk in their way, but we, poor mortals, in our present state, would probably find them precious slow company. Even mere good people are rather depressing. It is in our faults and failings, not in our virtues, that we touch one another and find sympathy. We differ widely enough in our nobler qualities. It is in our follies that we are at one. Some of us are pious, some of us are generous. Some few of us are honest, comparatively speaking; and some, fewer still, may possibly be truthful. But in vanity and kindred weaknesses we can all join hands. Vanity is one of those touches of nature that make the whole world kin. From the Indian hunter, proud of his belt of scalps, to the European general, swelling beneath his row of stars and medals; from the Chinese, gleeful at the length of his pigtail, to the "professional beauty," suffering tortures in order that her waist may resemble a peg-top; from draggle-tailed little Polly Stiggins, strutting through Seven Dials with a tattered parasol over her head, to the princess sweeping through a drawing-room with a train of four yards long; from 'Arry, winning by vulgar chaff the loud laughter of his pals, to the statesman whose ears are tickled by the cheers that greet his high-sounding periods; from the dark-skinned African, bartering his rare oils and ivory for a few glass beads to hang about his neck, to the Christian maiden selling her white body for a score of tiny stones and an empty title to tack before her name—all march, and fight, and bleed, and die beneath its tawdry flag.

Ay, ay, vanity is truly the motive-power that moves humanity, and it is flattery that greases the wheels. If you want to win affection and respect in this world, you must flatter people. Flatter high and low, and rich and poor, and silly and wise. You will get on famously. Praise this man's virtues and that man's vices. Compliment everybody upon everything, and especially upon what they haven't got. Admire guys for their beauty, fools for their wit, and boors for their breeding. Your discernment and intelligence will be extolled to the skies.

Every one can be got over by flattery. The belted earl—"belted earl" is the correct phrase, I believe. I don't know what it means, unless it be an earl that wears a belt instead of braces. Some men do. I don't like it myself. You have to keep the thing so tight for it to be of any use, and that is uncomfortable. Anyhow, whatever particular kind of an earl a belted earl may be, he is, I assert, get-overable by flattery; just as every other human being is, from a duchess to a cat's-meat man, from a plow boy to a poet—and the poet far easier than the plowboy, for butter sinks better into wheaten bread than into oaten cakes.

As for love, flattery is its very life-blood. Fill a person with love for themselves, and what runs over will be your share, says a certain witty and truthful Frenchman whose name I can't for the life of me remember. (Confound it! I never can remember names when I want to.) Tell a girl she is an angel, only more angelic than an angel; that she is a goddess, only more graceful, queenly, and heavenly than the average goddess; that she is more fairy-like than Titania, more beautiful than Venus, more enchanting than Parthenope; more adorable, lovely, and radiant, in short, than any other woman that ever did live, does live, or could live, and you will make a very favorable impression upon her trusting little heart. Sweet innocent! she will believe every word you say. It is so easy to deceive a woman—in this way.

Dear little souls, they hate flattery, so they tell you; and when you say, "Ah, darling, it isn't flattery in your case, it's plain, sober truth; you really are, without exaggeration, the most beautiful, the most good, the most charming, the most divine, the most perfect human creature that ever trod this earth," they will smile a quiet, approving smile, and, leaning against your manly shoulder, murmur that you are a dear good fellow after all.

By Jove! fancy a man trying to make love on strictly truthful principles, determining never to utter a word of mere compliment or hyperbole, but to scrupulously confine himself to exact fact! Fancy his gazing rapturously into his mistress' eyes and whispering softly to her that she wasn't, on the whole, bad-looking, as girls went! Fancy his holding up her little hand and assuring her that it was of a light drab color shot with red; and telling her as he pressed her to his heart that her nose, for a turned-up one, seemed rather pretty; and that her eyes appeared to him, as far as he could judge, to be quite up to the average standard of such things!

A nice chance he would stand against the man who would tell her that her face was like a fresh blush rose, that her hair was a wandering sunbeam imprisoned by her smiles, and her eyes like two evening stars.

There are various ways of flattering, and, of course, you must adapt your style to your subject. Some people like it laid on with a trowel, and this requires very little art. With sensible persons, however, it needs to be done very delicately, and more by suggestion than actual words. A good many like it wrapped up in the form of an insult, as—"Oh, you are a perfect fool, you are. You would give your last sixpence to the first hungry-looking beggar you met;" while others will swallow it only when administered through the medium of a third person, so that if C wishes to get at an A of this sort, he must confide to A's particular friend B that he thinks A a splendid fellow, and beg him, B, not to mention it, especially to A. Be careful that B is a reliable man, though, otherwise he won't.

Those fine, sturdy John Bulls who "hate flattery, sir," "Never let anybody get over me by flattery," etc., etc., are very simply managed. Flatter them enough upon their absence of vanity, and you can do what you like with them.

After all, vanity is as much a virtue as a vice. It is easy to recite copy-book maxims against its sinfulness, but it is a passion that can move us to good as well as to evil. Ambition is only vanity ennobled. We want to win praise and admiration—or fame as we prefer to name it—and so we write great books, and paint grand pictures, and sing sweet songs; and toil with willing hands in study, loom, and laboratory.

We wish to become rich men, not in order to enjoy ease and comfort—all that any one man can taste of those may be purchased anywhere for 200 pounds per annum—but that our houses may be bigger and more gaudily furnished than our neighbors'; that our horses and servants may be more numerous; that we may dress our wives and daughters in absurd but expensive clothes; and that we may give costly dinners of which we ourselves individually do not eat a shilling's worth. And to do this we aid the world's work with clear and busy brain, spreading commerce among its peoples, carrying civilization to its remotest corners.

Do not let us abuse vanity, therefore. Rather let us use it. Honor itself is but the highest form of vanity. The instinct is not confined solely to Beau Brummels and Dolly Vardens. There is the vanity of the peacock and the vanity of the eagle. Snobs are vain. But so, too, are heroes. Come, oh! my young brother bucks, let us be vain together. Let us join hands and help each other to increase our vanity. Let us be vain, not of our trousers and hair, but of brave hearts and working hands, of truth, of purity, of nobility. Let us be too vain to stoop to aught that is mean or base, too vain for petty selfishness and little-minded envy, too vain to say an unkind word or do an unkind act. Let us be vain of being single-hearted, upright gentlemen in the midst of a world of knaves. Let us pride ourselves upon thinking high thoughts, achieving great deeds, living good lives.

On Getting on in the World.

Not exactly the sort of thing for an idle fellow to think about, is it? But outsiders, you know, often see most of the game; and sitting in my arbor by the wayside, smoking my hookah of contentment and eating the sweet lotus-leaves of indolence, I can look out musingly upon the whirling throng that rolls and tumbles past me on the great high-road of life.

Never-ending is the wild procession. Day and night you can hear the quick tramp of the myriad feet—some running, some walking, some halting and lame; but all hastening, all eager in the feverish race, all straining life and limb and heart and soul to reach the ever-receding horizon of success.

Mark them as they surge along—men and women, old and young, gentle and simple, fair and foul, rich and poor, merry and sad—all hurrying, bustling, scrambling. The strong pushing aside the weak, the cunning creeping past the foolish; those behind elbowing those before; those in front kicking, as they run, at those behind. Look close and see the flitting show. Here is an old man panting for breath, and there a timid maiden driven by a hard and sharp-faced matron; here is a studious youth, reading "How to Get On in the World" and letting everybody pass him as he stumbles along with his eyes on his book; here is a bored-looking man, with a fashionably dressed woman jogging his elbow; here a boy gazing wistfully back at the sunny village that he never again will see; here, with a firm and easy step, strides a broad-shouldered man; and here, with stealthy tread, a thin-faced, stooping fellow dodges and shuffles upon his way; here, with gaze fixed always on the ground, an artful rogue carefully works his way from side to side of the road and thinks he is going forward; and here a youth with a noble face stands, hesitating as he looks from the distant goal to the mud beneath his feet.

And now into sight comes a fair girl, with her dainty face growing more wrinkled at every step, and now a care-worn man, and now a hopeful lad.

A motley throng—a motley throng! Prince and beggar, sinner and saint, butcher and baker and candlestick maker, tinkers and tailors, and plowboys and sailors—all jostling along together. Here the counsel in his wig and gown, and here the old Jew clothes-man under his dingy tiara; here the soldier in his scarlet, and here the undertaker's mute in streaming hat-band and worn cotton gloves; here the musty scholar fumbling his faded leaves, and here the scented actor dangling his showy seals. Here the glib politician crying his legislative panaceas, and here the peripatetic Cheap-Jack holding aloft his quack cures for human ills. Here the sleek capitalist and there the sinewy laborer; here the man of science and here the shoe-back; here the poet and here the water-rate collector; here the cabinet minister and there the ballet-dancer. Here a red-nosed publican shouting the praises of his vats and there a temperance lecturer at 50 pounds a night; here a judge and there a swindler; here a priest and there a gambler. Here a jeweled duchess, smiling and gracious; here a thin lodging-house keeper, irritable with cooking; and here a wabbling, strutting thing, tawdry in paint and finery.

Cheek by cheek they struggle onward. Screaming, cursing, and praying, laughing, singing, and moaning, they rush past side by side. Their speed never slackens, the race never ends. There is no wayside rest for them, no halt by cooling fountains, no pause beneath green shades. On, on, on—on through the heat and the crowd and the dust—on, or they will be trampled down and lost—on, with throbbing brain and tottering limbs—on, till the heart grows sick, and the eyes grow blurred, and a gurgling groan tells those behind they may close up another space.

And yet, in spite of the killing pace and the stony track, who but the sluggard or the dolt can hold aloof from the course? Who—like the belated traveler that stands watching fairy revels till he snatches and drains the goblin cup and springs into the whirling circle—can view the mad tumult and not be drawn into its midst? Not I, for one. I confess to the wayside arbor, the pipe of contentment, and the lotus-leaves being altogether unsuitable metaphors. They sounded very nice and philosophical, but I'm afraid I am not the sort of person to sit in arbors smoking pipes when there is any fun going on outside. I think I more resemble the Irishman who, seeing a crowd collecting, sent his little girl out to ask if there was going to be a row—"'Cos, if so, father would like to be in it."

I love the fierce strife. I like to watch it. I like to hear of people getting on in it—battling their way bravely and fairly—that is, not slipping through by luck or trickery. It stirs one's old Saxon fighting blood like the tales of "knights who fought 'gainst fearful odds" that thrilled us in our school-boy days.

And fighting the battle of life is fighting against fearful odds, too. There are giants and dragons in this nineteenth century, and the golden casket that they guard is not so easy to win as it appears in the story-books. There, Algernon takes one long, last look at the ancestral hall, dashes the tear-drop from his eye, and goes off—to return in three years' time, rolling in riches. The authors do not tell us "how it's done," which is a pity, for it would surely prove exciting.

But then not one novelist in a thousand ever does tell us the real story of their hero. They linger for a dozen pages over a tea-party, but sum up a life's history with "he had become one of our merchant princes," or "he was now a great artist, with the world at his feet." Why, there is more real life in one of Gilbert's patter-songs than in half the biographical novels ever written. He relates to us all the various steps by which his office-boy rose to be the "ruler of the queen's navee," and explains to us how the briefless barrister managed to become a great and good judge, "ready to try this breach of promise of marriage." It is in the petty details, not in the great results, that the interest of existence lies.

What we really want is a novel showing us all the hidden under-current of an ambitious man's career—his struggles, and failures, and hopes, his disappointments and victories. It would be an immense success. I am sure the wooing of Fortune would prove quite as interesting a tale as the wooing of any flesh-and-blood maiden, though, by the way, it would read extremely similar; for Fortune is, indeed, as the ancients painted her, very like a woman—not quite so unreasonable and inconsistent, but nearly so—and the pursuit is much the same in one case as in the other. Ben Jonson's couplet—

> "Court a mistress, she denies you;
> Let her alone, she will court you"—

puts them both in a nutshell. A woman never thoroughly cares for her lover until he has ceased to care for her; and it is not until you have snapped your fingers in Fortune's face and turned on your heel that she begins to smile upon you.

But by that time you do not much care whether she smiles or frowns. Why could she not have smiled when her smiles would have filled you with ecstasy? Everything comes too late in this world.

Good people say that it is quite right and proper that it should be so, and that it proves ambition is wicked.

Bosh! Good people are altogether wrong. (They always are, in my opinion. We never agree on any single point.) What would the world do without ambitious people, I should like to know? Why, it would be as flabby as a Norfolk dumpling. Ambitious people are the leaven which raises it into wholesome bread. Without ambitious people the world would never get up. They are busybodies who are about early in the morning, hammering, shouting, and rattling the fire-irons, and rendering it generally impossible for the rest of the house to remain in bed.

Wrong to be ambitious, forsooth! The men wrong who, with bent back and sweating brow, cut the smooth road over which humanity marches forward from generation to generation! Men wrong for using the talents that their Master has intrusted to them—for toiling while others play!

Of course they are seeking their reward. Man is not given that godlike unselfishness that thinks only of others' good. But in working for themselves they are working for us all. We are so bound together that no man can labor for himself alone. Each blow he strikes in his own behalf helps to mold the universe. The stream in struggling onward turns the mill-wheel; the coral insect, fashioning its tiny cell, joins continents to one another; and the ambitious man, building a pedestal for himself, leaves a monument to posterity. Alexander and Caesar fought for their own ends, but in doing so they put a belt of civilization half round the earth. Stephenson, to win a fortune, invented the steam-engine; and Shakespeare wrote his plays in order to keep a comfortable home for Mrs. Shakespeare and the little Shakespeares.

Contented, unambitious people are all very well in their way. They form a neat, useful background for great portraits to be painted against, and they make a respectable, if not particularly intelligent, audience for the active spirits of the age to play before. I have not a word to say against contented people so long as they keep quiet. But do not, for goodness' sake, let them go strutting about, as they are so fond of doing, crying out that they are the true models for the whole species. Why, they are the deadheads, the drones in the great hive, the street crowds that lounge about, gaping at those who are working.

And let them not imagine, either—as they are also fond of doing—that they are very wise and philosophical and that it is a very artful thing to be contented. It may be true that "a contented mind is happy anywhere," but so is a Jerusalem pony, and the consequence is that both are put anywhere and are treated anyhow. "Oh, you need not bother about him," is what is said; "he is very contented as he is, and it would be a pity to disturb him." And so your contented party is passed over and the discontented man gets his place.

If you are foolish enough to be contented, don't show it, but grumble with the rest; and if you can do with a little, ask for a great deal. Because if you don't you won't get any. In this world it is necessary to adopt the principle pursued by the plaintiff in an action for damages, and to demand ten times more than you are ready to accept. If you can feel satisfied with a hundred, begin by insisting on a thousand; if you start by suggesting a hundred you will only get ten.

It was by not following this simple plan that poor Jean Jacques Rousseau came to such grief. He fixed the summit of his earthly bliss at living in an orchard with an amiable woman and a cow, and he never attained even that. He did get as far as the orchard, but the woman was not amiable, and she brought her mother with her, and there was no cow. Now, if he had made up his mind for a large country estate, a houseful of angels, and a cattle-show, he might have lived to possess his kitchen garden and one head of live-stock, and even possibly have come across that *rara-avis*—a really amiable woman.

What a terribly dull affair, too, life must be for contented people! How heavy the time must hang upon their hands, and what on earth do they occupy their thoughts with, supposing that they have any? Reading the paper and smoking seems to be the intellectual food of the majority of them, to which the more energetic add playing the flute and talking about the affairs of the next-door neighbor.

They never knew the excitement of expectation nor the stern delight of accomplished effort, such as stir the pulse of the man who has objects, and hopes, and plans. To the ambitious man life is a brilliant game—a game that calls forth all his tact and energy and nerve—a game to be won, in the long run, by the quick eye and the steady hand, and yet having sufficient chance about its working out to give it all the glorious zest of uncertainty. He exults in it as the strong swimmer in the heaving billows, as the athlete in the wrestle, the soldier in the battle.

And if he be defeated he wins the grim joy of fighting; if he lose the race, he, at least, has had a run. Better to work and fail than to sleep one's life away.

So, walk up, walk up, walk up. Walk up, ladies and gentlemen! walk up, boys and girls! Show your skill and try your strength; brave your luck and prove your pluck. Walk up! The show is never closed and the game is always going. The only genuine sport in all the fair, gentlemen—highly respectable and strictly moral—patronized by the nobility, clergy, and gentry. Established in the year one, gentlemen, and been flourishing ever since—walk up! Walk up, ladies and gentlemen, and take a hand. There are prizes for all and all can play. There is gold for the man and fame for the boy; rank for the maiden and pleasure for the fool. So walk up, ladies and gentlemen, walk up!—all prizes and no blanks; for some few win, and as to the rest, why—

> "The rapture of pursuing
> Is the prize the vanquished gain."

On the Weather.

Things do go so contrary-like with me. I wanted to hit upon an especially novel, out-of-the-way subject for one of these articles. "I will write one paper about something altogether new," I said to myself; "something that nobody else has ever written or talked about before; and then I can have it all my own way." And I went about for days, trying to think of something of this kind; and I couldn't. And Mrs. Cutting, our charwoman, came yesterday—I don't mind mentioning her name, because I know she will not see this book. She would not look at such a frivolous publication. She never reads anything but the Bible and *Lloyd's Weekly News*. All other literature she considers unnecessary and sinful.

She said: "Lor', sir, you do look worried."

I said: "Mrs. Cutting, I am trying to think of a subject the discussion of which will come upon the world in the nature of a startler—some subject upon which no previous human being has ever said a word—some subject that will attract by its novelty, invigorate by its surprising freshness."

She laughed and said I was a funny gentleman.

That's my luck again. When I make serious observations people chuckle; when I attempt a joke nobody sees it. I had a beautiful one last week. I thought it so good, and I worked it up and brought it in artfully at a dinner-party. I forget how exactly, but we had been talking about the attitude of Shakespeare toward the Reformation, and I said something and immediately added, "Ah, that reminds me; such a funny thing happened the other day in Whitechapel." "Oh," said they, "what was that?" "Oh, 'twas awfully funny," I replied, beginning to giggle myself; "it will make you roar;" and I told it them.

There was dead silence when I finished—it was one of those long jokes, too—and then, at last, somebody said: "And that was the joke?"

I assured them that it was, and they were very polite and took my word for it. All but one old gentleman at the other end of the table, who wanted to know which was the joke—what he said to her or what she said to him; and we argued it out.

Some people are too much the other way. I knew a fellow once whose natural tendency to laugh at everything was so strong that if you wanted to talk seriously to him, you had to explain beforehand that what you were going to say would not be amusing. Unless you got him to clearly understand this, he would go off into fits of merriment over every word you uttered. I have known him on being asked the time stop short in the middle of the road, slap his leg, and burst into a roar of laughter. One never dared say anything really funny to that man. A good joke would have killed him on the spot.

In the present instance I vehemently repudiated the accusation of frivolity, and pressed Mrs. Cutting for practical ideas. She then became thoughtful and hazarded "samplers;" saying that she never heard them spoken much of now, but that they used to be all the rage when she was a girl.

I declined samplers and begged her to think again. She pondered a long while, with a tea-tray in her hands, and at last suggested the weather, which she was sure had been most trying of late.

And ever since that idiotic suggestion I have been unable to get the weather out of my thoughts or anything else in.

It certainly is most wretched weather. At all events it is so now at the time I am writing, and if it isn't particularly unpleasant when I come to be read it soon will be.

It always is wretched weather according to us. The weather is like the government—always in the wrong. In summer-time we say it is stifling; in winter that it is killing; in spring and autumn we find fault with it for being neither one thing nor the other and wish it would make up its mind. If it is fine we say the country is being ruined for want of rain; if it does rain we pray for fine weather. If December passes without snow, we indignantly demand to know what has become of our good old-fashioned winters, and talk as if we had been cheated out of something we had bought and paid for; and when it does snow, our language is a disgrace to a Christian nation. We shall never be content until each man makes his own weather and keeps it to himself.

If that cannot be arranged, we would rather do without it altogether.

Yet I think it is only to us in cities that all weather is so unwelcome. In her own home, the country, Nature is sweet in all her moods. What can be more beautiful than the snow, falling big with mystery in silent softness, decking the fields and trees with white as if for a fairy wedding! And how delightful is a walk when the frozen ground rings beneath our swinging tread—when our blood tingles in the rare keen air, and the sheep-dogs' distant bark and children's laughter peals faintly clear like Alpine bells across the open hills! And then skating! scudding with wings of steel across the swaying ice, making whirring music as we fly. And oh, how dainty is spring—Nature at sweet eighteen!

When the little hopeful leaves peep out so fresh and green, so pure and bright, like young lives pushing shyly out into the bustling world; when the fruit-tree blossoms, pink and white, like village maidens in their Sunday frocks, hide each whitewashed cottage in a cloud of fragile splendor; and the cuckoo's note upon the breeze is wafted through the woods! And summer, with its deep dark green and drowsy hum—when the rain-drops whisper solemn secrets to the listening leaves and the twilight lingers in the lanes! And autumn! ah, how sadly fair, with its golden glow and the dying grandeur of its tinted woods—its blood-red sunsets and its ghostly evening mists, with its busy murmur of reapers, and its laden orchards, and the calling of the gleaners, and the festivals of praise!

The very rain, and sleet, and hail seem only Nature's useful servants when found doing their simple duties in the country; and the East Wind himself is nothing worse than a boisterous friend when we meet him between the hedge-rows.

But in the city where the painted stucco blisters under the smoky sun, and the sooty rain brings slush and mud, and the snow lies piled in dirty heaps, and the chill blasts whistle down dingy streets and shriek round flaring gas lit corners, no face of Nature charms us. Weather in towns is like a skylark in a counting-house—out of place and in the way. Towns ought to be covered in, warmed by hot-water pipes, and lighted by electricity. The weather is a country lass and does not appear to advantage in town. We liked well enough to flirt with her in the hay-field, but she does not seem so fascinating when we meet her in Pall Mall. There is too much of her there. The frank, free laugh and hearty voice that sounded so pleasant in the dairy jars against the artificiality of town-bred life, and her ways become exceedingly trying.

Just lately she has been favoring us with almost incessant rain for about three weeks; and I am a demned damp, moist, unpleasant body, as Mr. Mantalini puts it.

Our next-door neighbor comes out in the back garden every now and then and says it's doing the country a world of good—not his coming out into the back garden, but the weather. He doesn't understand anything about it, but ever since he started a cucumber-frame last summer he has regarded himself in the light of an agriculturist, and talks in this absurd way with the idea of impressing the rest of the terrace with the notion that he is a retired farmer. I can only hope that for this once he is correct, and that the weather really is doing good to something, because it is doing me a considerable amount of damage. It is spoiling both my clothes and my temper. The latter I can afford, as I have a good supply of it, but it wounds me to the quick to see my dear old hats and trousers sinking, prematurely worn and aged, beneath the cold world's blasts and snows.

There is my new spring suit, too. A beautiful suit it was, and now it is hanging up so bespattered with mud I can't bear to look at it.

That was Jim's fault, that was. I should never have gone out in it that night if it had not been for him. I was just trying it on when he came in. He threw up his arms with a wild yell the moment he caught sight of it, and exclaimed that he had "got 'em again!"

I said: "Does it fit all right behind?"

"Spiffin, old man," he replied. And then he wanted to know if I was coming out.

I said "no" at first, but he overruled me. He said that a man with a suit like that had no right to stop indoors. "Every citizen," said he, "owes a duty to the public. Each one should contribute to the general happiness as far as lies in his power. Come out and give the girls a treat."

Jim is slangy. I don't know where he picks it up. It certainly is not from me.

I said: "Do you think it will really please 'em?" He said it would be like a day in the country to them.

That decided me. It was a lovely evening and I went.

When I got home I undressed and rubbed myself down with whisky, put my feet in hot water and a mustard-plaster on my chest, had a basin of gruel and a glass of hot brandy-and-water, tallowed my nose, and went to bed.

These prompt and vigorous measures, aided by a naturally strong constitution, were the means of preserving my life; but as for the suit! Well, there, it isn't a suit; it's a splash-board.

And I did fancy that suit, too. But that's just the way. I never do get particularly fond of anything in this world but what something dreadful happens to it. I had a tame rat when I was a boy, and I loved that animal as only a boy would love an old water-rat; and one day it fell into a large dish of gooseberry-fool that was standing to cool in the kitchen, and nobody knew what had become of the poor creature until the second helping.

I do hate wet weather in town. At least, it is not so much the wet as the mud that I object to. Somehow or other I seem to possess an irresistible alluring power over mud. I have only to show myself in the street on a muddy day to be half-smothered by it. It all comes of being so attractive, as the old lady said when she was struck by lightning. Other people can go out on dirty days and walk about for hours without getting a speck upon themselves; while if I go across the road I come back a perfect disgrace to be seen (as in my boyish days my poor dear mother tried often to tell me). If there were only one dab of mud to be found in the whole of London, I am convinced I should carry it off from all competitors.

I wish I could return the affection, but I fear I never shall be able to. I have a horror of what they call the "London particular." I feel miserable and muggy all through a dirty day, and it is quite a relief to pull one's clothes off and get into bed, out of the way of it all. Everything goes wrong in wet weather. I don't know how it is, but there always seem to me to be more people, and dogs, and perambulators, and cabs, and carts about in wet weather than at any other time, and they all get in your way more, and everybody is so disagreeable—except myself—and it does make me so wild. And then, too, somehow I always find myself carrying more things in wet weather than in dry; and when you have a bag, and three parcels, and a newspaper, and it suddenly comes on to rain, you can't open your umbrella.

Which reminds me of another phase of the weather that I can't bear, and that is April weather (so called because it always comes in May). Poets think it very nice. As it does not know its own mind five minutes together, they liken it to a woman; and it is supposed to be very charming on that account. I don't appreciate it, myself. Such lightning-change business may be all very agreeable in a girl. It is no doubt highly delightful to have to do with a person who grins one moment about nothing at all, and snivels the next for precisely the same cause, and who then giggles, and then sulks, and who is rude, and affectionate, and bad-tempered, and jolly, and boisterous, and silent, and passionate, and cold, and stand-offish, and flopping, all in one minute (mind, I don't say this. It is those poets. And they are supposed to be connoisseurs of this sort of thing); but in the weather the disadvantages of the system are more apparent. A woman's tears do not make one wet, but the rain does; and her coldness does not lay the foundations of asthma and rheumatism, as the east wind is apt to. I can prepare for and put up with a regularly bad day, but these ha'porth-of-all-sorts kind of days do not suit me. It aggravates me to see a bright blue sky above me when I am walking along wet through, and there is something so exasperating about the way the sun comes out smiling after a drenching shower, and seems to say: "Lord love you, you don't mean to say you're wet? Well, I am surprised. Why, it was only my fun."

They don't give you time to open or shut your umbrella in an English April, especially if it is an "automaton" one—the umbrella, I mean, not the April.

I bought an "automaton" once in April, and I did have a time with it! I wanted an umbrella, and I went into a shop in the Strand and told them so, and they said:

"Yes, sir. What sort of an umbrella would you like?"

I said I should like one that would keep the rain off, and that would not allow itself to be left behind in a railway carriage.

"Try an 'automaton,'" said the shopman.

"What's an 'automaton'?" said I.

"Oh, it's a beautiful arrangement," replied the man, with a touch of enthusiasm. "It opens and shuts itself."

I bought one and found that he was quite correct. It did open and shut itself. I had no control over it whatever. When it began to rain, which it did that season every alternate five minutes, I used to try and get the machine to open, but it would not budge; and then I used to stand and struggle with the wretched thing, and shake it, and swear at it, while the rain poured down in torrents. Then the moment the rain ceased the absurd thing would go up suddenly with a jerk and would not come down again; and I had to walk about under a bright blue sky, with an umbrella over my head, wishing that it would come on to rain again, so that it might not seem that I was insane.

When it did shut it did so unexpectedly and knocked one's hat off.

I don't know why it should be so, but it is an undeniable fact that there is nothing makes a man look so supremely ridiculous as losing his hat. The feeling of helpless misery that shoots down one's back on suddenly becoming aware that one's head is bare is among the most bitter ills that flesh is heir to. And then there is the wild chase after it, accompanied by an excitable small dog, who thinks it is a game, and in the course of which you are certain to upset three or four innocent children—to say nothing of their mothers—butt a fat old gentleman on to the top of a perambulator, and carom off a ladies' seminary into the arms of a wet sweep.

After this, the idiotic hilarity of the spectators and the disreputable appearance of the hat when recovered appear but of minor importance.

Altogether, what between March winds, April showers, and the entire absence of May flowers, spring is not a success in cities. It is all very well in the country, as I have said, but in towns whose population is anything over ten thousand it most certainly ought to be abolished. In the world's grim workshops it is like the children—out of place. Neither shows to advantage amid the dust and din. It seems so sad to see the little dirt-grimed brats try to play in the noisy courts and muddy streets. Poor little uncared-for, unwanted human atoms, they are not children. Children are bright-eyed, chubby, and shy. These are dingy, screeching elves, their tiny faces seared and withered, their baby laughter cracked and hoarse.

The spring of life and the spring of the year were alike meant to be cradled in the green lap of nature. To us in the town spring brings but its cold winds and drizzling rains. We must seek it among the leafless woods and the brambly lanes, on the heathy moors and the great still hills, if we want to feel its joyous breath and hear its silent voices. There is a glorious freshness in the spring there. The scurrying clouds, the open bleakness, the rushing wind, and the clear bright air thrill one with vague energies and hopes. Life, like the landscape around us, seems bigger, and wider, and freer—a rainbow road leading to unknown ends. Through the silvery rents that bar the sky we seem to catch a glimpse of the great hope and grandeur that lies around this little throbbing world, and a breath of its scent is wafted us on the wings of the wild March wind.

Strange thoughts we do not understand are stirring in our hearts. Voices are calling us to some great effort, to some mighty work. But we do not comprehend their meaning yet, and the hidden echoes within us that would reply are struggling, inarticulate and dumb.

We stretch our hands like children to the light, seeking to grasp we know not what. Our thoughts, like the boys' thoughts in the Danish song, are very long, long thoughts, and very vague; we cannot see their end.

It must be so. All thoughts that peer outside this narrow world cannot be else than dim and shapeless. The thoughts that we can clearly grasp are very little thoughts—that two and two make four-that when we are hungry it is pleasant to eat—that honesty is the best policy; all greater thoughts are undefined and vast to our poor childish brains. We see but dimly through the mists that roll around our time-girt isle of life, and only hear the distant surging of the great sea beyond.

On Cats and Dogs.

What I've suffered from them this morning no tongue can tell. It began with Gustavus Adolphus. Gustavus Adolphus (they call him "Gusty" down-stairs for short) is a very good sort of dog when he is in the middle of a large field or on a fairly extensive common, but I won't have him indoors. He means well, but this house is not his size. He stretches himself, and over go two chairs and a what-not. He wags his tail, and the room looks as if a devastating army had marched through it. He breathes, and it puts the fire out.

At dinner-time he creeps in under the table, lies there for awhile, and then gets up suddenly; the first intimation we have of his movements being given by the table, which appears animated by a desire to turn somersaults. We all clutch at it frantically and endeavor to maintain it in a horizontal position; whereupon his struggles, he being under the impression that some wicked conspiracy is being hatched against him, become fearful, and the final picture presented is generally that of an overturned table and a smashed-up dinner sandwiched between two sprawling layers of infuriated men and women.

He came in this morning in his usual style, which he appears to have founded on that of an American cyclone, and the first thing he did was to sweep my coffee-cup off the table with his tail, sending the contents full into the middle of my waistcoat.

I rose from my chair and approached him at a rapid rate. He preceded me in the direction of the door. At the door he met Eliza coming in with eggs. Eliza observed "Ugh!" and sat down on the floor, the eggs took up different positions about the carpet, where they spread themselves out, and Gustavus Adolphus left the room. I called after him, strongly advising him to go straight downstairs and not let me see him again for the next hour or so; and he seeming to agree with me, dodged the coal-scoop and went, while I returned, dried myself and finished breakfast. I made sure that he had gone in to the yard, but when I looked into the passage ten minutes later he was sitting at the top of the stairs. I ordered him down at once, but he only barked and jumped about, so I went to see what was the matter.

It was Tittums. She was sitting on the top stair but one and wouldn't let him pass.

Tittums is our kitten. She is about the size of a penny roll. Her back was up and she was swearing like a medical student.

She does swear fearfully. I do a little that way myself sometimes, but I am a mere amateur compared with her. To tell you the truth—mind, this is strictly between ourselves, please; I shouldn't like your wife to know I said it—the women folk don't understand these things; but between you and me, you know, I think it does a man good to swear. Swearing is the safety-valve through which the bad temper that might otherwise do serious internal injury to his mental mechanism escapes in harmless vaporing. When a man has said: "Bless you, my dear, sweet sir. What the sun, moon, and stars made you so careless (if I may be permitted the expression) as to allow your light and delicate foot to descend upon my corn with so much force? Is it that you are physically incapable of comprehending the direction in which you are proceeding? you nice, clever young man—you!" or words to that effect, he feels better. Swearing has the same soothing effect upon our angry passions that smashing the furniture or slamming the doors is so well known to exercise; added to which it is much cheaper. Swearing clears a man out like a pen'orth of gunpowder does the wash-house chimney. An occasional explosion is good for both. I rather distrust a man who never swears, or savagely kicks the foot-stool, or pokes the fire with unnecessary violence. Without some outlet, the anger caused by the ever-occurring troubles of life is apt to rankle and fester within. The petty annoyance, instead of being thrown from us, sits down beside us and becomes a sorrow, and the little offense is brooded over till, in the hot-bed of rumination, it grows into a great injury, under whose poisonous shadow springs up hatred and revenge.

Swearing relieves the feelings—that is what swearing does. I explained this to my aunt on one occasion, but it didn't answer with her. She said I had no business to have such feelings.

That is what I told Tittums. I told her she ought to be ashamed of herself, brought up in at Christian family as she was, too. I don't so much mind hearing an old cat swear, but I can't bear to see a mere kitten give way to it. It seems sad in one so young.

I put Tittums in my pocket and returned to my desk. I forgot her for the moment, and when I looked I found that she had squirmed out of my pocket on to the table and was trying to swallow the pen; then she put her leg into the ink-pot and upset it; then she licked her leg; then she swore again—at me this time.

I put her down on the floor, and there Tim began rowing with her. I do wish Tim would mind his own business. It was no concern of his what she had been doing. Besides, he is not a saint himself. He is only a two-year-old fox-terrier, and he interferes with everything and gives himself the airs of a gray-headed Scotch collie.

Tittums' mother has come in and Tim has got his nose scratched, for which I am remarkably glad. I have put them all three out in the passage, where they are fighting at the present moment. I'm in a mess with the ink and in a thundering bad temper; and if anything more in the cat or dog line comes fooling about me this morning, it had better bring its own funeral contractor with it.

Yet, in general, I like cats and dogs very much indeed. What jolly chaps they are! They are much superior to human beings as companions. They do not quarrel or argue with you. They never talk about themselves but listen to you while you talk about yourself, and keep up an appearance of being interested in the conversation. They never make stupid remarks. They never observe to Miss Brown across a dinner-table that they always understood she was very sweet on Mr. Jones (who has just married Miss Robinson). They never mistake your wife's cousin for her husband and fancy that you are the father-in-law. And they never ask a young author with fourteen tragedies, sixteen comedies, seven farces, and a couple of burlesques in his desk why he doesn't write a play.

They never say unkind things. They never tell us of our faults, "merely for our own good." They do not at inconvenient moments mildly remind us of our past follies and mistakes. They do not say, "Oh, yes, a lot of use you are if you are ever really wanted"—sarcastic like. They never inform us, like our *inamoratas* sometimes do, that we are not nearly so nice as we used to be. We are always the same to them.

They are always glad to see us. They are with us in all our humors. They are merry when we are glad, sober when we feel solemn, and sad when we are sorrowful.

"Halloo! happy and want a lark? Right you are; I'm your man. Here I am, frisking round you, leaping, barking, pirouetting, ready for any amount of fun and mischief. Look at my eyes if you doubt me. What shall it be? A romp in the drawing-room and never mind the furniture, or a scamper in the fresh, cool air, a scud across the fields and down the hill, and won't we let old Gaffer Goggles' geese know what time o' day it is, neither! Whoop! come along."

Or you'd like to be quiet and think. Very well. Pussy can sit on the arm of the chair and purr, and Montmorency will curl himself up on the rug and blink at the fire, yet keeping one eye on you the while, in case you are seized with any sudden desire in the direction of rats.

And when we bury our face in our hands and wish we had never been born, they don't sit up very straight and observe that we have brought it all upon ourselves. They don't even hope it will be a warning to us. But they come up softly and shove their heads against us. If it is a cat she stands on your shoulder, rumples your hair, and says, "Lor,' I am sorry for you, old man," as plain as words can speak; and if it is a dog he looks up at you with his big, true eyes and says with them, "Well you've always got me, you know. We'll go through the world together and always stand by each other, won't we?"

He is very imprudent, a dog is. He never makes it his business to inquire whether you are in the right or in the wrong, never bothers as to whether you are going up or down upon life's ladder, never asks whether you are rich or poor, silly or wise, sinner or saint. You are his pal. That is enough for him, and come luck or misfortune, good repute or bad, honor or shame, he is going to stick to you, to comfort you, guard you, and give his life for you if need be—foolish, brainless, soulless dog!

Ah! old stanch friend, with your deep, clear eyes and bright, quick glances, that take in all one has to say before one has time to speak it, do you know you are only an animal and have no mind? Do you know that that dull-eyed, gin-sodden lout leaning against the post out there is immeasurably your intellectual superior? Do you know that every little-minded, selfish scoundrel who lives by cheating and tricking, who never did a gentle deed or said a kind word, who never had a thought that was not mean and low or a desire that was not base, whose every action is a fraud, whose every utterance is a lie—do you know that these crawling skulks (and there are millions of them in the world), do you know they are all as much superior to you as the sun is superior to rushlight you honorable, brave-hearted, unselfish brute? They are MEN, you know, and MEN are the greatest, and noblest, and wisest, and best beings in the whole vast eternal universe. Any man will tell you that.

Yes, poor doggie, you are very stupid, very stupid indeed, compared with us clever men, who understand all about politics and philosophy, and who know everything, in short, except what we are and where we came from and whither we are going, and what everything outside this tiny world and most things in it are.

Never mind, though, pussy and doggie, we like you both all the better for your being stupid. We all like stupid things. Men can't bear clever women, and a woman's ideal man is some one she can call a "dear old stupid." It is so pleasant to come across people more stupid than ourselves. We love them at once for being so. The world must be rather a rough place for clever people. Ordinary folk dislike them, and as for themselves, they hate each other most cordially.

But there, the clever people are such a very insignificant minority that it really doesn't much matter if they are unhappy. So long as the foolish people can be made comfortable the world, as a whole, will get on tolerably well.

Cats have the credit of being more worldly wise than dogs—of looking more after their own interests and being less blindly devoted to those of their friends. And we men and women are naturally shocked at such selfishness. Cats certainly do love a family that has a carpet in the kitchen more than a family that has not; and if there are many children about, they prefer to spend their leisure time next door. But, taken altogether, cats are libeled. Make a friend of one, and she will stick to you through thick and thin. All the cats that I have had have been most firm comrades. I had a cat once that used to follow me about everywhere, until it even got quite embarrassing, and I had to beg her, as a personal favor, not to accompany me any further down the High Street. She used to sit up for me when I was late home and meet me in the passage. It made me feel quite like a married man, except that she never asked where I had been and then didn't believe me when I told her.

Another cat I had used to get drunk regularly every day. She would hang about for hours outside the cellar door for the purpose of sneaking in on the first opportunity and lapping up the drippings from the beer-cask. I do not mention this habit of hers in praise of the species, but merely to show how almost human some of them are. If the transmigration of souls is a fact, this animal was certainly qualifying most rapidly for a Christian, for her vanity was only second to her love of drink. Whenever she caught a particularly big rat, she would bring it up into the room where we were all sitting, lay the corpse down in the midst of us, and wait to be praised. Lord! how the girls used to scream.

Poor rats! They seem only to exist so that cats and dogs may gain credit for killing them and chemists make a fortune by inventing specialties in poison for their destruction. And yet there is something fascinating about them. There is a weirdness and uncanniness attaching to them. They are so cunning and strong, so terrible in their numbers, so cruel, so secret. They swarm in deserted houses, where the broken casements hang rotting to the crumbling walls and the doors swing creaking on their rusty hinges. They know the sinking ship and leave her, no one knows how or whither. They whisper to each other in their hiding-places how a doom will fall upon the hall and the great name die forgotten. They do fearful deeds in ghastly charnel-houses.

No tale of horror is complete without the rats. In stories of ghosts and murderers they scamper through the echoing rooms, and the gnawing of their teeth is heard behind the wainscot, and their gleaming eyes peer through the holes in the worm-eaten tapestry, and they scream in shrill, unearthly notes in the dead of night, while the moaning wind sweeps, sobbing, round the ruined turret towers, and passes wailing like a woman through the chambers bare and tenantless.

And dying prisoners, in their loathsome dungeons, see through the horrid gloom their small red eyes, like glittering coals, hear in the death-like silence the rush of their claw-like feet, and start up shrieking in the darkness and watch through the awful night.

I love to read tales about rats. They make my flesh creep so. I like that tale of Bishop Hatto and the rats. The wicked bishop, you know, had ever so much corn stored in his granaries and would not let the starving people touch it, but when they prayed to him for food gathered them together in his barn, and then shutting the doors on them, set fire to the place and burned them all to death. But next day there came thousands upon thousands of rats, sent to do judgment on him. Then Bishop Hatto fled to his strong tower that stood in the middle of the Rhine, and barred himself in and fancied he was safe. But the rats! they swam the river, they gnawed their way through the thick stone walls, and ate him alive where he sat.

> "They have whetted their teeth against the stones,
> And now they pick the bishop's bones;
> They gnawed the flesh from every limb,
> For they were sent to do judgment on him."

Oh, it's a lovely tale.

Then there is the story of the Pied Piper of Hamelin, how first he piped the rats away, and afterward, when the mayor broke faith with him, drew all the children along with him and went into the mountain. What a curious old legend that is! I wonder what it means, or has it any meaning at all? There seems something strange and deep lying hid beneath the rippling rhyme. It haunts me, that picture of the quaint, mysterious old piper piping through Hamelin's narrow streets, and the children following with dancing feet and thoughtful, eager faces. The old folks try to stay them, but the children pay no heed. They hear the weird, witched music and must follow. The games are left unfinished and the playthings drop from their careless hands. They know not whither they are hastening. The mystic music calls to them, and they follow, heedless and unasking where. It stirs and vibrates in their hearts and other sounds grow faint. So they wander through Pied Piper Street away from Hamelin town.

I get thinking sometimes if the Pied Piper is really dead, or if he may not still be roaming up and down our streets and lanes, but playing now so softly that only the children hear him. Why do the little faces look so grave and solemn when they pause awhile from romping, and stand, deep wrapt, with straining eyes? They only shake their curly heads and dart back laughing to their playmates when we question them. But I fancy myself they have been listening to the magic music of the old Pied Piper, and perhaps with those bright eyes of theirs have even seen his odd, fantastic figure gliding unnoticed through the whirl and throng.

Even we grown-up children hear his piping now and then. But the yearning notes are very far away, and the noisy, blustering world is always bellowing so loud it drowns the dreamlike melody. One day the sweet, sad strains will sound out full and clear, and then we too shall, like the little children, throw our playthings all aside and follow. The loving hands will be stretched out to stay us, and the voices we have learned to listen for will cry to us to stop. But we shall push the fond arms gently back and pass out through the sorrowing house and through the open door. For the wild, strange music will be ringing in our hearts, and we shall know the meaning of its song by then.

I wish people could love animals without getting maudlin over them, as so many do. Women are the most hardened offenders in such respects, but even our intellectual sex often degrade pets into nuisances by absurd idolatry. There are the gushing young ladies who, having read "David Copperfield," have thereupon sought out a small, longhaired dog of nondescript breed, possessed of an irritating habit of criticising a man's trousers, and of finally commenting upon the same by a sniff indicative of contempt and disgust. They talk sweet girlish prattle to this animal (when there is any one near enough to overhear them), and they kiss its nose, and put its unwashed head up against their cheek in a most touching manner; though I have noticed that these caresses are principally performed when there are young men hanging about.

Then there are the old ladies who worship a fat poodle, scant of breath and full of fleas. I knew a couple of elderly spinsters once who had a sort of German sausage on legs which they called a dog between them. They used to wash its face with warm water every morning. It had a mutton cutlet regularly for breakfast; and on Sundays, when one of the ladies went to church, the other always stopped at home to keep the dog company.

There are many families where the whole interest of life is centered upon the dog. Cats, by the way, rarely suffer from excess of adulation. A cat possesses a very fair sense of the ridiculous, and will put her paw down kindly but firmly upon any nonsense of this kind. Dogs, however, seem to like it. They encourage their owners in the tomfoolery, and the consequence is that in the circles I am speaking of what "dear Fido" has done, does do, will do, won't do, can do, can't do, was doing, is doing, is going to do, shall do, shan't do, and is about to be going to have done is the continual theme of discussion from morning till night.

All the conversation, consisting, as it does, of the very dregs of imbecility, is addressed to this confounded animal. The family sit in a row all day long, watching him, commenting upon his actions, telling each other anecdotes about him, recalling his virtues, and remembering with tears how one day they lost him for two whole hours, on which occasion he was brought home in a most brutal manner by the butcher-boy, who had been met carrying him by the scruff of his neck with one hand, while soundly cuffing his head with the other.

After recovering from these bitter recollections, they vie with each other in bursts of admiration for the brute, until some more than usually enthusiastic member, unable any longer to control his feelings, swoops down upon the unhappy quadruped in a frenzy of affection, clutches it to his heart, and slobbers over it. Whereupon the others, mad with envy, rise up, and seizing as much of the dog as the greed of the first one has left to them, murmur praise and devotion.

Among these people everything is done through the dog. If you want to make love to the eldest daughter, or get the old man to lend you the garden roller, or the mother to subscribe to the Society for the Suppression of Solo-Cornet Players in Theatrical Orchestras (it's a pity there isn't one, anyhow), you have to begin with the dog. You must gain its approbation before they will even listen to you, and if, as is highly probable, the animal, whose frank, doggy nature has been warped by the unnatural treatment he has received, responds to your overtures of friendship by viciously snapping at you, your cause is lost forever.

"If Fido won't take to any one," the father has thoughtfully remarked beforehand, "I say that man is not to be trusted. You know, Maria, how often I have said that. Ah! he knows, bless him."

Drat him!

And to think that the surly brute was once an innocent puppy, all legs and head, full of fun and play, and burning with ambition to become a big, good dog and bark like mother.

Ah me! life sadly changes us all. The world seems a vast horrible grinding machine, into which what is fresh and bright and pure is pushed at one end, to come out old and crabbed and wrinkled at the other.

Look even at Pussy Sobersides, with her dull, sleepy glance, her grave, slow walk, and dignified, prudish airs; who could ever think that once she was the blue-eyed, whirling, scampering, head-over-heels, mad little firework that we call a kitten?

What marvelous vitality a kitten has. It is really something very beautiful the way life bubbles over in the little creatures. They rush about, and mew, and spring; dance on their hind legs, embrace everything with their front ones, roll over and over, lie on their backs and kick. They don't know what to do with themselves, they are so full of life.

Can you remember, reader, when you and I felt something of the same sort of thing? Can you remember those glorious days of fresh young manhood—how, when coming home along the moonlit road, we felt too full of life for sober walking, and had to spring and skip, and wave our arms, and shout till belated farmers' wives thought—and with good reason, too—that we were mad, and kept close to the hedge, while we stood and laughed aloud to see them scuttle off so fast and made their blood run cold with a wild parting whoop, and the tears came, we knew not why? Oh, that magnificent young LIFE! that crowned us kings of the earth; that rushed through every tingling vein till we seemed to walk on air; that thrilled through our throbbing brains and told us to go forth and conquer the whole world; that welled up in our young hearts till we longed to stretch out our arms and gather all the toiling men and women and the little children to our breast and love them all—all. Ah! they were grand days, those deep, full days, when our coming life, like an unseen organ, pealed strange, yearnful music in our ears, and our young blood cried out like a war-horse for the battle. Ah, our pulse beats slow and steady now, and our old joints are rheumatic, and we love our easy-chair and pipe and sneer at boys' enthusiasm. But oh for one brief moment of that god-like life again!

On Being Shy.

All great literary men are shy. I am myself, though I am told it is hardly noticeable.

I am glad it is not. It used to be extremely prominent at one time, and was the cause of much misery to myself and discomfort to every one about me—my lady friends especially complained most bitterly about it.

A shy man's lot is not a happy one. The men dislike him, the women despise him, and he dislikes and despises himself. Use brings him no relief, and there is no cure for him except time; though I once came across a delicious recipe for overcoming the misfortune. It appeared among the "answers to correspondents" in a small weekly journal and ran as follows—I have never forgotten it: "Adopt an easy and pleasing manner, especially toward ladies."

Poor wretch! I can imagine the grin with which he must have read that advice. "Adopt an easy and pleasing manner, especially toward ladies," forsooth! Don't you adopt anything of the kind, my dear young shy friend. Your attempt to put on any other disposition than your own will infallibly result in your becoming ridiculously gushing and offensively familiar. Be your own natural self, and then you will only be thought to be surly and stupid.

The shy man does have some slight revenge upon society for the torture it inflicts upon him. He is able, to a certain extent, to communicate his misery. He frightens other people as much as they frighten him. He acts like a damper upon the whole room, and the most jovial spirits become in his presence depressed and nervous.

This is a good deal brought about by misunderstanding. Many people mistake the shy man's timidity for overbearing arrogance and are awed and insulted by it. His awkwardness is resented as insolent carelessness, and when, terror-stricken at the first word addressed to him, the blood rushes to his head and the power of speech completely fails him, he is regarded as an awful example of the evil effects of giving way to passion.

But, indeed, to be misunderstood is the shy man's fate on every occasion; and whatever impression he endeavors to create, he is sure to convey its opposite. When he makes a joke, it is looked upon as a pretended relation of fact and his want of veracity much condemned. His sarcasm is accepted as his literal opinion and gains for him the reputation of being an ass, while if, on the other hand, wishing to ingratiate himself, he ventures upon a little bit of flattery, it is taken for satire and he is hated ever afterward.

These and the rest of a shy man's troubles are always very amusing to other people, and have afforded material for comic writing from time immemorial. But if we look a little deeper we shall find there is a pathetic, one might almost say a tragic, side to the picture. A shy man means a lonely man—a man cut off from all companionship, all sociability. He moves about the world, but does not mix with it. Between him and his fellow-men there runs ever an impassable barrier—a strong, invisible wall that, trying in vain to scale, he but bruises himself against. He sees the pleasant faces and hears the pleasant voices on the other side, but he cannot stretch his hand across to grasp another hand. He stands watching the merry groups, and he longs to speak and to claim kindred with them. But they pass him by, chatting gayly to one another, and he cannot stay them. He tries to reach them, but his prison walls move with him and hem him in on every side. In the busy street, in the crowded room, in the grind of work, in the whirl of pleasure, amid the many or amid the few—wherever men congregate together, wherever the music of human speech is heard and human thought is flashed from human eyes, there, shunned and solitary, the shy man, like a leper, stands apart. His soul is full of love and longing, but the world knows it not. The iron mask of shyness is riveted before his face, and the man beneath is never seen. Genial words and hearty greetings are ever rising to his lips, but they die away in unheard whispers behind the steel clamps. His heart aches for the weary brother, but his sympathy is dumb. Contempt and indignation against wrong choke up his throat, and finding no safety-valve whence in passionate utterance they may burst forth, they only turn in again and harm him. All the hate and scorn and love of a deep nature such as the shy man is ever cursed by fester and corrupt within, instead of spending themselves abroad, and sour him into a misanthrope and cynic.

Yes, shy men, like ugly women, have a bad time of it in this world, to go through which with any comfort needs the hide of a rhinoceros. Thick skin is, indeed, our moral clothes, and without it we are not fit to be seen about in civilized society. A poor gasping, blushing creature, with trembling knees and twitching hands, is a painful sight to every one, and if it cannot cure itself, the sooner it goes and hangs itself the better.

The disease can be cured. For the comfort of the shy, I can assure them of that from personal experience. I do not like speaking about myself, as may have been noticed, but in the cause of humanity I on this occasion will do so, and will confess that at one time I was, as the young man in the Bab Ballad says, "the shyest of the shy," and "whenever I was introduced to any pretty maid, my knees they knocked together just as if I was afraid." Now, I would—nay, have—on this very day before yesterday I did the deed. Alone and entirely by myself (as the school-boy said in translating the "Bellum Gallicum") did I beard a railway refreshment-room young lady in her own lair. I rebuked her in terms of mingled bitterness and sorrow for her callousness and want of condescension. I insisted, courteously but firmly, on being accorded that deference and attention that was the right of the traveling Briton, and at the end I looked her full in the face. Need I say more?

True, immediately after doing so I left the room with what may possibly have appeared to be precipitation and without waiting for any refreshment. But that was because I had changed my mind, not because I was frightened, you understand.

One consolation that shy folk can take unto themselves is that shyness is certainly no sign of stupidity. It is easy enough for bull-headed clowns to sneer at nerves, but the highest natures are not necessarily those containing the greatest amount of moral brass. The horse is not an inferior animal to the cock-sparrow, nor the deer of the forest to the pig. Shyness simply means extreme sensibility, and has nothing whatever to do with self-consciousness or with conceit, though its relationship to both is continually insisted upon by the poll-parrot school of philosophy.

Conceit, indeed, is the quickest cure for it. When it once begins to dawn upon you that you are a good deal cleverer than any one else in this world, bashfulness becomes shocked and leaves you. When you can look round a roomful of people and think that each one is a mere child in intellect compared with yourself you feel no more shy of them than you would of a select company of magpies or orang-outangs.

Conceit is the finest armor that a man can wear. Upon its smooth, impenetrable surface the puny dagger-thrusts of spite and envy glance harmlessly aside. Without that breast-plate the sword of talent cannot force its way through the battle of life, for blows have to be borne as well as dealt. I do not, of course, speak of the conceit that displays itself in an elevated nose and a falsetto voice. That is not real conceit—that is only playing at being conceited; like children play at being kings and queens and go strutting about with feathers and long trains. Genuine conceit does not make a man objectionable. On the contrary, it tends to make him genial, kind-hearted, and simple. He has no need of affectation—he is far too well satisfied with his own character; and his pride is too deep-seated to appear at all on the outside. Careless alike of praise or blame, he can afford to be truthful. Too far, in fancy, above the rest of mankind to trouble about their petty distinctions, he is equally at home with duke or costermonger. And valuing no one's standard but his own, he is never tempted to practice that miserable pretense that less self-reliant people offer up as an hourly sacrifice to the god of their neighbor's opinion.

The shy man, on the other hand, is humble—modest of his own judgment and over-anxious concerning that of others. But this in the case of a young man is surely right enough. His character is unformed. It is slowly evolving itself out of a chaos of doubt and disbelief. Before the growing insight and experience the diffidence recedes. A man rarely carries his shyness past the hobbledehoy period. Even if his own inward strength does not throw it off, the rubbings of the world generally smooth it down. You scarcely ever meet a really shy man—except in novels or on the stage, where, by the bye, he is much admired, especially by the women.

There, in that supernatural land, he appears as a fair-haired and saintlike young man—fair hair and goodness always go together on the stage. No respectable audience would believe in one without the other. I knew an actor who mislaid his wig once and had to rush on to play the hero in his own hair, which was jet-black, and the gallery howled at all his noble sentiments under the impression that he was the villain. He—the shy young man—loves the heroine, oh so devotedly (but only in asides, for he dare not tell her of it), and he is so noble and unselfish, and speaks in such a low voice, and is so good to his mother; and the bad people in the play, they laugh at him and jeer at him, but he takes it all so gently, and in the end it transpires that he is such a clever man, though nobody knew it, and then the heroine tells him she loves him, and he is so surprised, and oh, so happy! and everybody loves him and asks him to forgive them, which he does in a few well-chosen and sarcastic words, and blesses them; and he seems to have generally such a good time of it that all the young fellows who are not shy long to be shy. But the really shy man knows better. He knows that it is not quite so pleasant in reality. He is not quite so interesting there as in the fiction. He is a little more clumsy and stupid and a little less devoted and gentle, and his hair is much darker, which, taken altogether, considerably alters the aspect of the case.

The point where he does resemble his ideal is in his faithfulness. I am fully prepared to allow the shy young man that virtue: he is constant in his love. But the reason is not far to seek. The fact is it exhausts all his stock of courage to look one woman in the face, and it would be simply impossible for him to go through the ordeal with a second. He stands in far too much dread of the whole female sex to want to go gadding about with many of them. One is quite enough for him.

Now, it is different with the young man who is not shy. He has temptations which his bashful brother never encounters. He looks around and everywhere sees roguish eyes and laughing lips. What more natural than that amid so many roguish ayes and laughing lips he should become confused and, forgetting for the moment which particular pair of roguish ayes and laughing lips it is that he belongs to, go off making love to the wrong set. The shy man, who never looks at anything but his own boots, sees not and is not tempted. Happy shy man!

Not but what the shy man himself would much rather not be happy in that way. He longs to "go it" with the others, and curses himself every day for not being able to. He will now and again, screwing up his courage by a tremendous effort, plunge into roguishness. But it is always a terrible *fiasco*, and after one or two feeble flounders he crawls out again, limp and pitiable.

I say "pitiable," though I am afraid he never is pitied. There are certain misfortunes which, while inflicting a vast amount of suffering upon their victims, gain for them no sympathy. Losing an umbrella, falling in love, toothache, black eyes, and having your hat sat upon may be mentioned as a few examples, but the chief of them all is shyness. The shy man is regarded as an animate joke. His tortures are the sport of the drawing-room arena and are pointed out and discussed with much gusto.

"Look," cry his tittering audience to each other; "he's blushing!"

"Just watch his legs," says one.

"Do you notice how he is sitting?" adds another: "right on the edge of the chair."

"Seems to have plenty of color," sneers a military-looking gentleman.

"Pity he's got so many hands," murmurs an elderly lady, with her own calmly folded on her lap. "They quite confuse him."

"A yard or two off his feet wouldn't be a disadvantage," chimes in the comic man, "especially as he seems so anxious to hide them."

And then another suggests that with such a voice he ought to have been a sea-captain. Some draw attention to the desperate way in which he is grasping his hat. Some comment upon his limited powers of conversation. Others remark upon the troublesome nature of his cough. And so on, until his peculiarities and the company are both thoroughly exhausted.

His friends and relations make matters still more unpleasant for the poor boy (friends and relations are privileged to be more disagreeable than other people). Not content with making fun of him among themselves, they insist on his seeing the joke. They mimic and caricature him for his own edification. One, pretending to imitate him, goes outside and comes in again in a ludicrously nervous manner, explaining to him afterward that that is the way he—meaning the shy fellow—walks into a room; or, turning to him with "This is the way you shake hands," proceeds to go through a comic pantomime with the rest of the room, taking hold of every one's hand as if it were a hot plate and flabbily dropping it again. And then they ask him why he blushes, and why he stammers, and why he always speaks in an almost inaudible tone, as if they thought he did it on purpose. Then one of them, sticking out his chest and strutting about the room like a pouter-pigeon, suggests quite seriously that that is the style he should adopt. The old man slaps him on the back and says: "Be bold, my boy. Don't be afraid of any one." The mother says, "Never do anything that you need be ashamed of, Algernon, and then you never need be ashamed of anything you do," and, beaming mildly at him, seems surprised at the clearness of her own logic. The boys tell him that he's "worse than a girl," and the girls repudiate the implied slur upon their sex by indignantly exclaiming that they are sure no girl would be half as bad.

They are quite right; no girl would be. There is no such thing as a shy woman, or, at all events, I have never come across one, and until I do I shall not believe in them. I know that the generally accepted belief is quite the reverse. All women are supposed to be like timid, startled fawns, blushing and casting down their gentle eyes when looked at and running away when spoken to; while we man are supposed to be a bold and rollicky lot, and the poor dear little women admire us for it, but are terribly afraid of us. It is a pretty theory, but, like most generally accepted theories, mere nonsense. The girl of twelve is self-contained and as cool as the proverbial cucumber, while her brother of twenty stammers and stutters by her side. A woman will enter a concert-room late, interrupt the performance, and disturb the whole audience without moving a hair, while her husband follows her, a crushed heap of apologizing misery.

The superior nerve of women in all matters connected with love, from the casting of the first sheep's-eye down to the end of the honeymoon, is too well acknowledged to need comment. Nor is the example a fair one to cite in the present instance, the positions not being equally balanced. Love is woman's business, and in "business" we all lay aside our natural weaknesses—the shyest man I ever knew was a photographic tout.

On Babies.

Oh, yes, I do—I know a lot about 'em. I was one myself once, though not long—not so long as my clothes. They were very long, I recollect, and always in my way when I wanted to kick. Why do babies have such yards of unnecessary clothing? It is not a riddle. I really want to know. I never could understand it. Is it that the parents are ashamed of the size of the child and wish to make believe that it is longer than it actually is? I asked a nurse once why it was. She said:

"Lor', sir, they always have long clothes, bless their little hearts."

And when I explained that her answer, although doing credit to her feelings, hardly disposed of my difficulty, she replied:

"Lor', sir, you wouldn't have 'em in short clothes, poor little dears?" And she said it in a tone that seemed to imply I had suggested some unmanly outrage.

Since than I have felt shy at making inquiries on the subject, and the reason—if reason there be—is still a mystery to me. But indeed, putting them in any clothes at all seems absurd to my mind. Goodness knows there is enough of dressing and undressing to be gone through in life without beginning it before we need; and one would think that people who live in bed might at all events be spared the torture. Why wake the poor little wretches up in the morning to take one lot of clothes off, fix another lot on, and put them to bed again, and then at night haul them out once more, merely to change everything back? And when all is done, what difference is there, I should like to know, between a baby's night-shirt and the thing it wears in the day-time?

Very likely, however, I am only making myself ridiculous—I often do, so I am informed—and I will therefore say no more upon this matter of clothes, except only that it would be of great convenience if some fashion were adopted enabling you to tell a boy from a girl.

At present it is most awkward. Neither hair, dress, nor conversation affords the slightest clew, and you are left to guess. By some mysterious law of nature you invariably guess wrong, and are thereupon regarded by all the relatives and friends as a mixture of fool and knave, the enormity of alluding to a male babe as "she" being only equaled by the atrocity of referring to a female infant as "he". Whichever sex the particular child in question happens not to belong to is considered as beneath contempt, and any mention of it is taken as a personal insult to the family.

And as you value your fair name do not attempt to get out of the difficulty by talking of "it."

There are various methods by which you may achieve ignominy and shame. By murdering a large and respected family in cold blood and afterward depositing their bodies in the water companies' reservoir, you will gain much unpopularity in the neighborhood of your crime, and even robbing a church will get you cordially disliked, especially by the vicar. But if you desire to drain to the dregs the fullest cup of scorn and hatred that a fellow human creature can pour out for you, let a young mother hear you call dear baby "it."

Your best plan is to address the article as "little angel." The noun "angel" being of common gender suits the case admirably, and the epithet is sure of being favorably received. "Pet" or "beauty" are useful for variety's sake, but "angel" is the term that brings you the greatest credit for sense and good-feeling. The word should be preceded by a short giggle and accompanied by as much smile as possible. And whatever you do, don't forget to say that the child has got its father's nose. This "fetches" the parents (if I may be allowed a vulgarism) more than anything. They will pretend to laugh at the idea at first and will say, "Oh, nonsense!" You must then get excited and insist that it is a fact. You need have no conscientious scruples on the subject, because the thing's nose really does resemble its father's—at all events quite as much as it does anything else in nature—being, as it is, a mere smudge.

Do not despise these hints, my friends. There may come a time when, with mamma on one side and grand mamma on the other, a group of admiring young ladies (not admiring you, though) behind, and a bald-headed dab of humanity in front, you will be extremely thankful for some idea of what to say. A man—an unmarried man, that is—is never seen to such disadvantage as when undergoing the ordeal of "seeing baby." A cold shudder runs down his back at the bare proposal, and the sickly smile with which he says how delighted he shall be ought surely to move even a mother's heart, unless, as I am inclined to believe, the whole proceeding is a mere device adopted by wives to discourage the visits of bachelor friends.

It is a cruel trick, though, whatever its excuse may be. The bell is rung and somebody sent to tell nurse to bring baby down. This is the signal for all the females present to commence talking "baby," during which time you are left to your own sad thoughts and the speculations upon the practicability of suddenly recollecting an important engagement, and the likelihood of your being believed if you do. Just when you have concocted an absurdly implausible tale about a man outside, the door opens, and a tall, severe-looking woman enters, carrying what at first sight appears to be a particularly skinny bolster, with the feathers all at one end. Instinct, however, tells you that this is the baby, and you rise with a miserable attempt at appearing eager. When the first gush of feminine enthusiasm with which the object in question is received has died out, and the number of ladies talking at once has been reduced to the ordinary four or five, the circle of fluttering petticoats divides, and room is made for you to step forward. This you do with much the same air that you would walk into the dock at Bow Street, and then, feeling unutterably miserable, you stand solemnly staring at the child. There is dead silence, and you know that every one is waiting for you to speak. You try to think of something to say, but find, to your horror, that your reasoning faculties have left you. It is a moment of despair, and your evil genius, seizing the opportunity, suggests to you some of the most idiotic remarks that it is possible for a human being to perpetrate. Glancing round with an imbecile smile, you sniggeringly observe that "it hasn't got much hair has it?" Nobody answers you for a minute, but at last the stately nurse says with much gravity:

"It is not customary for children five weeks old to have long hair." Another silence follows this, and you feel you are being given a second chance, which you avail yourself of by inquiring if it can walk yet, or what they feed it on.

By this time you have got to be regarded as not quite right in your head, and pity is the only thing felt for you. The nurse, however, is determined that, insane or not, there shall be no shirking and that you shall go through your task to the end. In the tones of a high priestess directing some religious mystery she says, holding the bundle toward you:

"Take her in your arms, sir." You are too crushed to offer any resistance and so meekly accept the burden. "Put your arm more down her middle, sir," says the high-priestess, and then all step back and watch you intently as though you were going to do a trick with it.

What to do you know no more than you did what to say. It is certain something must be done, and the only thing that occurs to you is to heave the unhappy infant up and down to the accompaniment of "oopsee-daisy," or some remark of equal intelligence. "I wouldn't jig her, sir, if I were you," says the nurse; "a very little upsets her." You promptly decide not to jig her and sincerely hope that you have not gone too far already.

At this point the child itself, who has hitherto been regarding you with an expression of mingled horror and disgust, puts an end to the nonsense by beginning to yell at the top of its voice, at which the priestess rushes forward and snatches it from you with "There! there! there! What did ums do to ums?" "How very extraordinary!" you say pleasantly. "Whatever made it go off like that?" "Oh, why, you must have done something to her!" says the mother indignantly; "the child wouldn't scream like that for nothing." It is evident they think you have been running pins into it.

The brat is calmed at last, and would no doubt remain quiet enough, only some mischievous busybody points you out again with "Who's this, baby?" and the intelligent child, recognizing you, howls louder than ever.

Whereupon some fat old lady remarks that "it's strange how children take a dislike to any one." "Oh, they know," replies another mysteriously. "It's a wonderful thing," adds a third; and then everybody looks sideways at you, convinced you are a scoundrel of the blackest dye; and they glory in the beautiful idea that your true character, unguessed by your fellow-men, has been discovered by the untaught instinct of a little child.

Babies, though, with all their crimes and errors, are not without their use—not without use, surely, when they fill an empty heart; not without use when, at their call, sunbeams of love break through care-clouded faces; not without use when their little fingers press wrinkles into smiles.

Odd little people! They are the unconscious comedians of the world's great stage. They supply the humor in life's all-too-heavy drama. Each one, a small but determined opposition to the order of things in general, is forever doing the wrong thing at the wrong time, in the wrong place and in the wrong way. The nurse-girl who sent Jenny to see what Tommy and Totty were doing and "tell 'em they mustn't" knew infantile nature. Give an average baby a fair chance, and if it doesn't do something it oughtn't to a doctor should be called in at once.

They have a genius for doing the most ridiculous things, and they do them in a grave, stoical manner that is irresistible. The business-like air with which two of them will join hands and proceed due east at a break-neck toddle, while an excitable big sister is roaring for them to follow her in a westerly direction, is most amusing—except, perhaps, for the big sister. They walk round a soldier, staring at his legs with the greatest curiosity, and poke him to see if he is real. They stoutly maintain, against all argument and much to the discomfort of the victim, that the bashful young man at the end of the 'bus is "dadda." A crowded street-corner suggests itself to their minds as a favorable spot for the discussion of family affairs at a shrill treble. When in the middle of crossing the road they are seized with a sudden impulse to dance, and the doorstep of a busy shop is the place they always select for sitting down and taking off their shoes.

When at home they find the biggest walking-stick in the house or an umbrella—open preferred-of much assistance in getting upstairs. They discover that they love Mary Ann at the precise moment when that faithful domestic is blackleading the stove, and nothing will relieve their feelings but to embrace her then and there. With regard to food, their favorite dishes are coke and cat's meat. They nurse pussy upside down, and they show their affection for the dog by pulling his tail.

They are a deal of trouble, and they make a place untidy and they cost a lot of money to keep; but still you would not have the house without them. It would not be home without their noisy tongues and their mischief-making hands. Would not the rooms seem silent without their pattering feet, and might not you stray apart if no prattling voices called you together?

It should be so, and yet I have sometimes thought the tiny hand seemed as a wedge, dividing. It is a bearish task to quarrel with that purest of all human affections—that perfecting touch to a woman's life—a mother's love. It is a holy love, that we coarser-fibered men can hardly understand, and I would not be deemed to lack reverence for it when I say that surely it need not swallow up all other affection. The baby need not take your whole heart, like the rich man who walled up the desert well. Is there not another thirsty traveler standing by?

In your desire to be a good mother, do not forget to be a good wife. No need for all the thought and care to be only for one. Do not, whenever poor Edwin wants you to come out, answer indignantly, "What, and leave baby!" Do not spend all your evenings upstairs, and do not confine your conversation exclusively to whooping-cough and measles. My dear little woman, the child is not going to die every time it sneezes, the house is not bound to get burned down and the nurse run away with a soldier every time you go outside the front door; nor the cat sure to come and sit on the precious child's chest the moment you leave the bedside. You worry yourself a good deal too much about that solitary chick, and you worry everybody else too. Try and think of your other duties, and your pretty face will not be always puckered into wrinkles, and there will be cheerfulness in the parlor as well as in the nursery. Think of your big baby a little. Dance him about a bit; call him pretty names; laugh at him now and then. It is only the first baby that takes up the whole of a woman's time. Five or six do not require nearly so much attention as one. But before then the mischief has been done. A house where there seems no room for him and a wife too busy to think of him have lost their hold on that so unreasonable husband of yours, and he has learned to look elsewhere for comfort and companionship.

But there, there, there! I shall get myself the character of a baby-hater if I talk any more in this strain. And Heaven knows I am not one. Who could be, to look into the little innocent faces clustered in timid helplessness round those great gates that open down into the world?

The world—the small round world! what a vast mysterious place it must seem to baby eyes! What a trackless continent the back garden appears! What marvelous explorations they make in the cellar under the stairs! With what awe they gaze down the long street, wondering, like us bigger babies when we gaze up at the stars, where it all ends!

And down that longest street of all—that long, dim street of life that stretches out before them—what grave, old-fashioned looks they seem to cast! What pitiful, frightened looks sometimes! I saw a little mite sitting on a doorstep in a Soho slum one night, and I shall never forget the look that the gas-lamp showed me on its wizen face—a look of dull despair, as if from the squalid court the vista of its own squalid life had risen, ghostlike, and struck its heart dead with horror.

Poor little feet, just commencing the stony journey! We old travelers, far down the road, can only pause to wave a hand to you. You come out of the dark mist, and we, looking back, see you, so tiny in the distance, standing on the brow of the hill, your arms stretched out toward us. God speed you! We would stay and take your little hands in ours, but the murmur of the great sea is in our ears and we may not linger. We must hasten down, for the shadowy ships are waiting to spread their sable sails.

On Eating and Drinking.

I always was fond of eating and drinking, even as a child—especially eating, in those early days. I had an appetite then, also a digestion. I remember a dull-eyed, livid-complexioned gentleman coming to dine at our house once. He watched me eating for about five minutes, quite fascinated seemingly, and then he turned to my father with—

"Does your boy ever suffer from dyspepsia?"

"I never heard him complain of anything of that kind," replied my father. "Do you ever suffer from dyspepsia, Colly wobbles?" (They called me Colly wobbles, but it was not my real name.)

"No, pa," I answered. After which I added:

"What is dyspepsia, pa?"

My livid-complexioned friend regarded me with a look of mingled amazement and envy. Then in a tone of infinite pity he slowly said:

"You will know—some day."

My poor, dear mother used to say she liked to see me eat, and it has always been a pleasant reflection to me since that I must have given her much gratification in that direction. A growing, healthy lad, taking plenty of exercise and careful to restrain himself from indulging in too much study, can generally satisfy the most exacting expectations as regards his feeding powers.

It is amusing to see boys eat when you have not got to pay for it. Their idea of a square meal is a pound and a half of roast beef with five or six good-sized potatoes (soapy ones preferred as being more substantial), plenty of greens, and four thick slices of Yorkshire pudding, followed by a couple of currant dumplings, a few green apples, a pen'orth of nuts, half a dozen jumbles, and a bottle of ginger-beer. After that they play at horses.

How they must despise us men, who require to sit quiet for a couple of hours after dining off a spoonful of clear soup and the wing of a chicken!

But the boys have not all the advantages on their side. A boy never enjoys the luxury of being satisfied. A boy never feels full. He can never stretch out his legs, put his hands behind his head, and, closing his eyes, sink into the ethereal blissfulness that encompasses the well-dined man. A dinner makes no difference whatever to a boy. To a man it is as a good fairy's potion, and after it the world appears a brighter and a better place. A man who has dined satisfactorily experiences a yearning love toward all his fellow-creatures. He strokes the cat quite gently and calls it "poor pussy," in tones full of the tenderest emotion. He sympathizes with the members of the German band outside and wonders if they are cold; and for the moment he does not even hate his wife's relations.

A good dinner brings out all the softer side of a man. Under its genial influence the gloomy and morose become jovial and chatty. Sour, starchy individuals, who all the rest of the day go about looking as if they lived on vinegar and Epsom salts, break out into wreathed smiles after dinner, and exhibit a tendency to pat small children on the head and to talk to them—vaguely—about sixpences. Serious men thaw and become mildly cheerful, and snobbish young men of the heavy-mustache type forget to make themselves objectionable.

I always feel sentimental myself after dinner. It is the only time when I can properly appreciate love-stories. Then, when the hero clasps "her" to his heart in one last wild embrace and stifles a sob, I feel as sad as though I had dealt at whist and turned up only a deuce; and when the heroine dies in the end I weep. If I read the same tale early in the morning I should sneer at it. Digestion, or rather indigestion, has a marvelous effect upon the heart. If I want to write any thing very pathetic—I mean, if I want to try to write anything very pathetic—I eat a large plateful of hot buttered muffins about an hour beforehand, and then by the time I sit down to my work a feeling of unutterable melancholy has come over me. I picture heartbroken lovers parting forever at lonely wayside stiles, while the sad twilight deepens around them, and only the tinkling of a distant sheep-bell breaks the sorrow-laden silence. Old men sit and gaze at withered flowers till their sight is dimmed by the mist of tears. Little dainty maidens wait and watch at open casements; but "he cometh not," and the heavy years roll by and the sunny gold tresses wear white and thin. The babies that they dandled have become grown men and women with podgy torments of their own, and the playmates that they laughed with are lying very silent under the waving grass. But still they wait and watch, till the dark shadows of the unknown night steal up and gather round them and the world with its childish troubles fades from their aching eyes.

I see pale corpses tossed on white-foamed waves, and death-beds stained with bitter tears, and graves in trackless deserts. I hear the wild wailing of women, the low moaning of little children, the dry sobbing of strong men. It's all the muffins. I could not conjure up one melancholy fancy upon a mutton chop and a glass of champagne.

A full stomach is a great aid to poetry, and indeed no sentiment of any kind can stand upon an empty one. We have not time or inclination to indulge in fanciful troubles until we have got rid of our real misfortunes. We do not sigh over dead dicky-birds with the bailiff in the house, and when we do not know where on earth to get our next shilling from, we do not worry as to whether our mistress' smiles are cold, or hot, or lukewarm, or anything else about them.

Foolish people—when I say "foolish people" in this contemptuous way I mean people who entertain different opinions to mine. If there is one person I do despise more than another, it is the man who does not think exactly the same on all topics as I do—foolish people, I say, then, who have never experienced much of either, will tell you that mental distress is far more agonizing than bodily. Romantic and touching theory! so comforting to the love-sick young sprig who looks down patronizingly at some poor devil with a white starved face and thinks to himself, "Ah, how happy you are compared with me!"—so soothing to fat old gentlemen who cackle about the superiority of poverty over riches. But it is all nonsense—all cant. An aching head soon makes one forget an aching heart. A broken finger will drive away all recollections of an empty chair. And when a man feels really hungry he does not feel anything else.

We sleek, well-fed folk can hardly realize what feeling hungry is like. We know what it is to have no appetite and not to care for the dainty victuals placed before us, but we do not understand what it means to sicken for food—to die for bread while others waste it—to gaze with famished eyes upon coarse fare steaming behind dingy windows, longing for a pen'orth of pea pudding and not having the penny to buy it—to feel that a crust would be delicious and that a bone would be a banquet.

Hunger is a luxury to us, a piquant, flavor-giving sauce. It is well worth while to get hungry and thirsty merely to discover how much gratification can be obtained from eating and drinking. If you wish to thoroughly enjoy your dinner, take a thirty-mile country walk after breakfast and don't touch anything till you get back. How your eyes will glisten at sight of the white table-cloth and steaming dishes then! With what a sigh of content you will put down the empty beer tankard and take up your knife and fork! And how comfortable you feel afterward as you push back your chair, light a cigar, and beam round upon everybody.

Make sure, however, when adopting this plan, that the good dinner is really to be had at the end, or the disappointment is trying. I remember once a friend and I—dear old Joe, it was. Ah! how we lose one another in life's mist. It must be eight years since I last saw Joseph Taboys. How pleasant it would be to meet his jovial face again, to clasp his strong hand, and to hear his cheery laugh once more! He owes me 14 shillings, too. Well, we were on a holiday together, and one morning we had breakfast early and started for a tremendous long walk. We had ordered a duck for dinner over night. We said, "Get a big one, because we shall come home awfully hungry;" and as we were going out our landlady came up in great spirits. She said, "I have got you gentlemen a duck, if you like. If you get through that you'll do well;" and she held up a bird about the size of a door-mat. We chuckled at the sight and said we would try. We said it with self-conscious pride, like men who know their own power. Then we started.

We lost our way, of course. I always do in the country, and it does make me so wild, because it is no use asking direction of any of the people you meet. One might as well inquire of a lodging-house slavey the way to make beds as expect a country bumpkin to know the road to the next village. You have to shout the question about three times before the sound of your voice penetrates his skull. At the third time he slowly raises his head and stares blankly at you. You yell it at him then for a fourth time, and he repeats it after you. He ponders while you count a couple of hundred, after which, speaking at the rate of three words a minute, he fancies you "couldn't do better than—" Here he catches sight of another idiot coming down the road and bawls out to him the particulars, requesting his advice. The two then argue the case for a quarter of an hour or so, and finally agree that you had better go straight down the lane, round to the right and cross by the third stile, and keep to the left by old Jimmy Milcher's cow-shed, and across the seven-acre field, and through the gate by Squire Grubbin's hay-stack, keeping the bridle-path for awhile till you come opposite the hill where the windmill used to be—but it's gone now—and round to the right, leaving Stiggin's plantation behind you; and you say "Thank you" and go away with a splitting headache, but without the faintest notion of your way, the only clear idea you have on the subject being that somewhere or other there is a stile which has to be got over; and at the next turn you come upon four stiles, all leading in different directions!

We had undergone this ordeal two or three times. We had tramped over fields. We had waded through brooks and scrambled over hedges and walls. We had had a row as to whose fault it was that we had first lost our way. We had got thoroughly disagreeable, footsore, and weary. But throughout it all the hope of that duck kept us up. A fairy-like vision, it floated before our tired eyes and drew us onward. The thought of it was as a trumpet-call to the fainting. We talked of it and cheered each other with our recollections of it. "Come along," we said; "the duck will be spoiled."

We felt a strong temptation, at one point, to turn into a village inn as we passed and have a cheese and a few loaves between us, but we heroically restrained ourselves: we should enjoy the duck all the better for being famished.

We fancied we smelled it when we go into the town and did the last quarter of a mile in three minutes. We rushed upstairs, and washed ourselves, and changed our clothes, and came down, and pulled our chairs up to the table, and sat and rubbed our hands while the landlady removed the covers, when I seized the knife and fork and started to carve.

It seemed to want a lot of carving. I struggled with it for about five minutes without making the slightest impression, and then Joe, who had been eating potatoes, wanted to know if it wouldn't be better for some one to do the job that understood carving. I took no notice of his foolish remark, but attacked the bird again; and so vigorously this time that the animal left the dish and took refuge in the fender.

We soon had it out of that, though, and I was prepared to make another effort. But Joe was getting unpleasant. He said that if he had thought we were to have a game of blind hockey with the dinner he would have got a bit of bread and cheese outside.

I was too exhausted to argue. I laid down the knife and fork with dignity and took a side seat and Joe went for the wretched creature. He worked away in silence for awhile, and then he muttered "Damn the duck" and took his coat off.

We did break the thing up at length with the aid of a chisel, but it was perfectly impossible to eat it, and we had to make a dinner off the vegetables and an apple tart. We tried a mouthful of the duck, but it was like eating India-rubber.

It was a wicked sin to kill that drake. But there! there's no respect for old institutions in this country.

I started this paper with the idea of writing about eating and drinking, but I seem to have confined my remarks entirely to eating as yet. Well, you see, drinking is one of those subjects with which it is inadvisable to appear too well acquainted. The days are gone by when it was considered manly to go to bed intoxicated every night, and a clear head and a firm hand no longer draw down upon their owner the reproach of effeminacy. On the contrary, in these sadly degenerate days an evil-smelling breath, a blotchy face, a reeling gait, and a husky voice are regarded as the hall marks of the cad rather than or the gentleman.

Even nowadays, though, the thirstiness of mankind is something supernatural. We are forever drinking on one excuse or another. A man never feels comfortable unless he has a glass before him. We drink before meals, and with meals, and after meals. We drink when we meet a friend, also when we part from a friend. We drink when we are talking, when we are reading, and when we are thinking. We drink one another's healths and spoil our own. We drink the queen, and the army, and the ladies, and everybody else that is drinkable; and I believe if the supply ran short we should drink our mothers-in-law.

By the way, we never eat anybody's health, always drink it. Why should we not stand up now and then and eat a tart to somebody's success?

To me, I confess the constant necessity of drinking under which the majority of men labor is quite unaccountable. I can understand people drinking to drown care or to drive away maddening thoughts well enough. I can understand the ignorant masses loving to soak themselves in drink—oh, yes, it's very shocking that they should, of course—very shocking to us who live in cozy homes, with all the graces and pleasures of life around us, that the dwellers in damp cellars and windy attics should creep from their dens of misery into the warmth and glare of the public-house bar, and seek to float for a brief space away from their dull world upon a Lethe stream of gin.

But think, before you hold up your hands in horror at their ill-living, what "life" for these wretched creatures really means. Picture the squalid misery of their brutish existence, dragged on from year to year in the narrow, noisome room where, huddled like vermin in sewers, they welter, and sicken, and sleep; where dirt-grimed children scream and fight and sluttish, shrill-voiced women cuff, and curse, and nag; where the street outside teems with roaring filth and the house around is a bedlam of riot and stench.

Think what a sapless stick this fair flower of life must be to them, devoid of mind and soul. The horse in his stall scents the sweet hay and munches the ripe corn contentedly. The watch-dog in his kennel blinks at the grateful sun, dreams of a glorious chase over the dewy fields, and wakes with a yelp of gladness to greet a caressing hand. But the clod-like life of these human logs never knows one ray of light. From the hour when they crawl from their comfortless bed to the hour when they lounge back into it again they never live one moment of real life. Recreation, amusement, companionship, they know not the meaning of. Joy, sorrow, laughter, tears, love, friendship, longing, despair, are idle words to them. From the day when their baby eyes first look out upon their sordid world to the day when, with an oath, they close them forever and their bones are shoveled out of sight, they never warm to one touch of human sympathy, never thrill to a single thought, never start to a single hope. In the name of the God of mercy; let them pour the maddening liquor down their throats and feel for one brief moment that they live!

Ah! we may talk sentiment as much as we like, but the stomach is the real seat of happiness in this world. The kitchen is the chief temple wherein we worship, its roaring fire is our vestal flame, and the cook is our great high-priest. He is a mighty magician and a kindly one. He soothes away all sorrow and care. He drives forth all enmity, gladdens all love. Our God is great and the cook is his prophet. Let us eat, drink, and be merry.

On Furnished Apartments.

"Oh, you have some rooms to let."

"Mother!"

"Well, what is it?"

"'Ere's a gentleman about the rooms."

"Ask 'im in. I'll be up in a minute."

"Will yer step inside, sir? Mother'll be up in a minute."

So you step inside and after a minute "mother" comes slowly up the kitchen stairs, untying her apron as she comes and calling down instructions to some one below about the potatoes.

"Good-morning, sir," says "mother," with a washed-out smile. "Will you step this way, please?"

"Oh, it's hardly worth while my coming up," you say. "What sort of rooms are they, and how much?"

"Well," says the landlady, "if you'll step upstairs I'll show them to you."

So with a protesting murmur, meant to imply that any waste of time complained of hereafter must not be laid to your charge, you follow "mother" upstairs.

At the first landing you run up against a pail and a broom, whereupon "mother" expatiates upon the unreliability of servant-girls, and bawls over the balusters for Sarah to come and take them away at once. When you get outside the rooms she pauses, with her hand upon the door, to explain to you that they are rather untidy just at present, as the last lodger left only yesterday; and she also adds that this is their cleaning-day—it always is. With this understanding you enter, and both stand solemnly feasting your eyes upon the scene before you. The rooms cannot be said to appear inviting. Even "mother's" face betrays no admiration. Untenanted "furnished apartments" viewed in the morning sunlight do not inspire cheery sensations. There is a lifeless air about them. It is a very different thing when you have settled down and are living in them. With your old familiar household gods to greet your gaze whenever you glance up, and all your little knick-knacks spread around you—with the photos of all the girls that you have loved and lost ranged upon the mantel-piece, and half a dozen disreputable-looking pipes scattered about in painfully prominent positions—with one carpet slipper peeping from beneath the coal-box and the other perched on the top of the piano—with the well-known pictures to hide the dingy walls, and these dear old friends, your books, higgledy-piggledy all over the place—with the bits of old blue china that your mother prized, and the screen she worked in those far by-gone days, when the sweet old face was laughing and young, and the white soft hair tumbled in gold-brown curls from under the coal-scuttle bonnet—

Ah, old screen, what a gorgeous personage you must have been in your young days, when the tulips and roses and lilies (all growing from one stem) were fresh in their glistening sheen! Many a summer and winter have come and gone since then, my friend, and you have played with the dancing firelight until you have grown sad and gray. Your brilliant colors are fast fading now, and the envious moths have gnawed your silken threads. You are withering away like the dead hands that wove you. Do you ever think of those dead hands? You seem so grave and thoughtful sometimes that I almost think you do. Come, you and I and the deep-glowing embers, let us talk together. Tell me in your silent language what you remember of those young days, when you lay on my little mother's lap and her girlish fingers played with your rainbow tresses. Was there never a lad near sometimes—never a lad who would seize one of those little hands to smother it with kisses, and who would persist in holding it, thereby sadly interfering with the progress of your making? Was not your frail existence often put in jeopardy by this same clumsy, headstrong lad, who would toss you disrespectfully aside that he—not satisfied with one—might hold both hands and gaze up into the loved eyes? I can see that lad now through the haze of the flickering twilight. He is an eager bright-eyed boy, with pinching, dandy shoes and tight-fitting smalls, snowy shirt frill and stock, and—oh! such curly hair. A wild, light-hearted boy! Can he be the great, grave gentleman upon whose stick I used to ride crosslegged, the care-worn man into whose thoughtful face I used to gaze with childish reverence and whom I used to call "father?" You say "yes," old screen; but are you quite sure? It is a serious charge you are bringing. Can it be possible? Did he have to kneel down in those wonderful smalls and pick you up and rearrange you before he was forgiven and his curly head smoothed by my mother's little hand? Ah! old screen, and did the lads and the lassies go making love fifty years ago just as they do now? Are men and women so unchanged? Did little maidens' hearts beat the same under pearl-embroidered bodices as they do under Mother Hubbard cloaks? Have steel casques and chimney-pot hats made no difference to the brains that work beneath them? Oh, Time! great Chronos! and is this your power? Have you dried up seas and leveled mountains and left the tiny human heart-strings to defy you? Ah, yes! they were spun by a Mightier than thou, and they stretch beyond your narrow ken, for their ends are made fast in eternity. Ay, you may mow down the leaves and the blossoms, but the roots of life lie too deep for your sickle to sever. You refashion Nature's garments, but you cannot vary by a jot the throbbings of her pulse. The world rolls round obedient to your laws, but the heart of man is not of your kingdom, for in its birthplace "a thousand years are but as yesterday."

I am getting away, though, I fear, from my "furnished apartments," and I hardly know how to get back. But I have some excuse for my meanderings this time. It is a piece of old furniture that has led me astray, and fancies gather, somehow, round old furniture, like moss around old stones. One's chairs and tables get to be almost part of one's life and to seem like quiet friends. What strange tales the wooden-headed old fellows could tell did they but choose to speak! At what unsuspected comedies and tragedies have they not assisted! What bitter tears have been sobbed into that old sofa cushion! What passionate whisperings the settee must have overheard!

New furniture has no charms for me compared with old. It is the old things that we love—the old faces, the old books, the old jokes. New furniture can make a palace, but it takes old furniture to make a home. Not merely old in itself—lodging-house furniture generally is that—but it must be old to us, old in associations and recollections. The furniture of furnished apartments, however ancient it may be in reality, is new to our eyes, and we feel as though we could never get on with it. As, too, in the case of all fresh acquaintances, whether wooden or human (and there is very little difference between the two species sometimes), everything impresses you with its worst aspect. The knobby wood-work and shiny horse-hair covering of the easy-chair suggest anything but ease. The mirror is smoky. The curtains want washing. The carpet is frayed. The table looks as if it would go over the instant anything was rested on it. The grate is cheerless, the wall-paper hideous. The ceiling appears to have had coffee spilt all over it, and the ornaments—well, they are worse than the wallpaper.

There must surely be some special and secret manufactory for the production of lodging-house ornaments. Precisely the same articles are to be found at every lodging-house all over the kingdom, and they are never seen anywhere else. There are the two—what do you call them? they stand one at each end of the mantel-piece, where they are never safe, and they are hung round with long triangular slips of glass that clank against one another and make you nervous. In the commoner class of rooms these works of art are supplemented by a couple of pieces of china which might each be meant to represent a cow sitting upon its hind legs, or a model of the temple of Diana at Ephesus, or a dog, or anything else you like to fancy. Somewhere about the room you come across a bilious-looking object, which at first you take to be a lump of dough left about by one of the children, but which on scrutiny seems to resemble an underdone cupid. This thing the landlady calls a statue. Then there is a "sampler" worked by some idiot related to the family, a picture of the "Huguenots," two or three Scripture texts, and a highly framed and glazed certificate to the effect that the father has been vaccinated, or is an Odd Fellow, or something of that sort.

You examine these various attractions and then dismally ask what the rent is.

"That's rather a good deal," you say on hearing the figure.

"Well, to tell you the truth," answers the landlady with a sudden burst of candor, "I've always had" (mentioning a sum a good deal in excess of the first-named amount), "and before that I used to have" (a still higher figure).

What the rent of apartments must have been twenty years ago makes one shudder to think of. Every landlady makes you feel thoroughly ashamed of yourself by informing you, whenever the subject crops up, that she used to get twice as much for her rooms as you are paying. Young men lodgers of the last generation must have been of a wealthier class than they are now, or they must have ruined themselves. I should have had to live in an attic.

Curious, that in lodgings the rule of life is reversed. The higher you get up in the world the lower you come down in your lodgings. On the lodging-house ladder the poor man is at the top, the rich man underneath. You start in the attic and work your way down to the first floor.

A good many great men have lived in attics and some have died there. Attics, says the dictionary, are "places where lumber is stored," and the world has used them to store a good deal of its lumber in at one time or another. Its preachers and painters and poets, its deep-browed men who will find out things, its fire-eyed men who will tell truths that no one wants to hear—these are the lumber that the world hides away in its attics. Haydn grew up in an attic and Chatterton starved in one. Addison and Goldsmith wrote in garrets. Faraday and De Quincey knew them well. Dr. Johnson camped cheerfully in them, sleeping soundly—too soundly sometimes—upon their trundle-beds, like the sturdy old soldier of fortune that he was, inured to hardship and all careless of himself. Dickens spent his youth among them, Morland his old age—alas! a drunken, premature old age. Hans Andersen, the fairy king, dreamed his sweet fancies beneath their sloping roofs. Poor, wayward-hearted Collins leaned his head upon their crazy tables; priggish Benjamin Franklin; Savage, the wrong-headed, much troubled when he could afford any softer bed than a doorstep; young Bloomfield, "Bobby" Burns, Hogarth, Watts the engineer—the roll is endless. Ever since the habitations of men were reared two stories high has the garret been the nursery of genius.

No one who honors the aristocracy of mind can feel ashamed of acquaintanceship with them. Their damp-stained walls are sacred to the memory of noble names. If all the wisdom of the world and all its art—all the spoils that it has won from nature, all the fire that it has snatched from heaven—were gathered together and divided into heaps, and we could point and say, for instance, these mighty truths were flashed forth in the brilliant *salon* amid the ripple of light laughter and the sparkle of bright eyes; and this deep knowledge was dug up in the quiet study, where the bust of Pallas looks serenely down on the leather-scented shelves; and this heap belongs to the crowded street; and that to the daisied field—the heap that would tower up high above the rest as a mountain above hills would be the one at which we should look up and say: this noblest pile of all—these glorious paintings and this wondrous music, these trumpet words, these solemn thoughts, these daring deeds, they were forged and fashioned amid misery and pain in the sordid squalor of the city garret. There, from their eyries, while the world heaved and throbbed below, the kings of men sent forth their eagle thoughts to wing their flight through the ages. There, where the sunlight streaming through the broken panes fell on rotting boards and crumbling walls; there, from their lofty thrones, those rag-clothed Joves have hurled their thunderbolts and shaken, before now, the earth to its foundations.

Huddle them up in your lumber-rooms, oh, world! Shut them fast in and turn the key of poverty upon them. Weld close the bars, and let them fret their hero lives away within the narrow cage. Leave them there to starve, and rot, and die. Laugh at the frenzied beatings of their hands against the door. Roll onward in your dust and noise and pass them by, forgotten.

But take care lest they turn and sting you. All do not, like the fabled phoenix, warble sweet melodies in their agony; sometimes they spit venom—venom you must breathe whether you will or no, for you cannot seal their mouths, though you may fetter their limbs. You can lock the door upon them, but they burst open their shaky lattices and call out over the house-tops so that men cannot but hear. You hounded wild Rousseau into the meanest garret of the Rue St. Jacques and jeered at his angry shrieks. But the thin, piping tones swelled a hundred years later into the sullen roar of the French Revolution, and civilization to this day is quivering to the reverberations of his voice.

As for myself, however, I like an attic. Not to live in: as residences they are inconvenient. There is too much getting up and down stairs connected with them to please me. It puts one unpleasantly in mind of the tread-mill. The form of the ceiling offers too many facilities for bumping your head and too few for shaving. And the note of the tomcat as he sings to his love in the stilly night outside on the tiles becomes positively distasteful when heard so near.

No, for living in give me a suit of rooms on the first floor of a Piccadilly mansion (I wish somebody would!); but for thinking in let me have an attic up ten flights of stairs in the densest quarter of the city. I have all Herr Teufelsdrockh's affection for attics. There is a sublimity about their loftiness. I love to "sit at ease and look down upon the wasps' nest beneath;" to listen to the dull murmur of the human tide ebbing and flowing ceaselessly through the narrow streets and lanes below. How small men seem, how like a swarm of ants sweltering in endless confusion on their tiny hill! How petty seems the work on which they are hurrying and skurrying! How childishly they jostle against one another and turn to snarl and scratch! They jabber and screech and curse, but their puny voices do not reach up here. They fret, and fume, and rage, and pant, and die; "but I, mein Werther, sit above it all; I am alone with the stars."

The most extraordinary attic I ever came across was one a friend and I once shared many years ago. Of all eccentrically planned things, from Bradshaw to the maze at Hampton Court, that room was the most eccentric. The architect who designed it must have been a genius, though I cannot help thinking that his talents would have been better employed in contriving puzzles than in shaping human habitations. No figure in Euclid could give any idea of that apartment. It contained seven corners, two of the walls sloped to a point, and the window was just over the fireplace. The only possible position for the bedstead was between the door and the cupboard. To get anything out of the cupboard we had to scramble over the bed, and a large percentage of the various commodities thus obtained was absorbed by the bedclothes. Indeed, so many things were spilled and dropped upon the bed that toward night-time it had become a sort of small cooperative store. Coal was what it always had most in stock. We used to keep our coal in the bottom part of the cupboard, and when any was wanted we had to climb over the bed, fill a shovelful, and then crawl back. It was an exciting moment when we reached the middle of the bed. We would hold our breath, fix our eyes upon the shovel, and poise ourselves for the last move. The next instant we, and the coals, and the shovel, and the bed would be all mixed up together.

I've heard of the people going into raptures over beds of coal. We slept in one every night and were not in the least stuck up about it.

But our attic, unique though it was, had by no means exhausted the architect's sense of humor. The arrangement of the whole house was a marvel of originality. All the doors opened outward, so that if any one wanted to leave a room at the same moment that you were coming downstairs it was unpleasant for you. There was no ground-floor—its ground-floor belonged to a house in the next court, and the front door opened direct upon a flight of stairs leading down to the cellar. Visitors on entering the house would suddenly shoot past the person who had answered the door to them and disappear down these stairs. Those of a nervous temperament used to imagine that it was a trap laid for them, and would shout murder as they lay on their backs at the bottom till somebody came and picked them up.

It is a long time ago now that I last saw the inside of an attic. I have tried various floors since but I have not found that they have made much difference to me. Life tastes much the same, whether we quaff it from a golden goblet or drink it out of a stone mug. The hours come laden with the same mixture of joy and sorrow, no matter where we wait for them. A waistcoat of broadcloth or of fustian is alike to an aching heart, and we laugh no merrier on velvet cushions than we did on wooden chairs. Often have I sighed in those low-ceilinged rooms, yet disappointments have come neither less nor lighter since I quitted them. Life works upon a compensating balance, and the happiness we gain in one direction we lose in another. As our means increase, so do our desires; and we ever stand midway between the two. When we reside in an attic we enjoy a supper of fried fish and stout. When we occupy the first floor it takes an elaborate dinner at the Continental to give us the same amount of satisfaction.

On Dress and Deportment.

They say—people who ought to be ashamed of themselves do—that the consciousness of being well dressed imparts a blissfulness to the human heart that religion is powerless to bestow. I am afraid these cynical persons are sometimes correct. I know that when I was a very young man (many, many years ago, as the story-books say) and wanted cheering up, I used to go and dress myself in all my best clothes. If I had been annoyed in any manner—if my washerwoman had discharged me, for instance; or my blank-verse poem had been returned for the tenth time, with the editor's compliments "and regrets that owing to want of space he is unable to avail himself of kind offer;" or I had been snubbed by the woman I loved as man never loved before—by the way, it's really extraordinary what a variety of ways of loving there must be. We all do it as it was never done before. I don't know how our great-grandchildren will manage. They will have to do it on their heads by their time if they persist in not clashing with any previous method.

Well, as I was saying, when these unpleasant sort of things happened and I felt crushed, I put on all my best clothes and went out. It brought back my vanishing self-esteem. In a glossy new hat and a pair of trousers with a fold down the front (carefully preserved by keeping them under the bed—I don't mean on the floor, you know, but between the bed and the mattress), I felt I was somebody and that there were other washerwomen: ay, and even other girls to love, and who would perhaps appreciate a clever, good-looking young fellow. I didn't care; that was my reckless way. I would make love to other maidens. I felt that in those clothes I could do it.

They have a wonderful deal to do with courting, clothes have. It is half the battle. At all events, the young man thinks so, and it generally takes him a couple of hours to get himself up for the occasion. His first half-hour is occupied in trying to decide whether to wear his light suit with a cane and drab billycock, or his black tails with a chimney-pot hat and his new umbrella. He is sure to be unfortunate in either decision. If he wears his light suit and takes the stick it comes on to rain, and he reaches the house in a damp and muddy condition and spends the evening trying to hide his boots. If, on the other hand, he decides in favor of the top hat and umbrella—nobody would ever dream of going out in a top hat without an umbrella; it would be like letting baby (bless it!) toddle out without its nurse. How I do hate a top hat! One lasts me a very long while, I can tell you. I only wear it when—well, never mind when I wear it. It lasts me a very long while.

I've had my present one five years. It was rather old-fashioned last summer, but the shape has come round again now and I look quite stylish.

But to return to our young man and his courting. If he starts off with the top hat and umbrella the afternoon turns out fearfully hot, and the perspiration takes all the soap out of his mustache and converts the beautifully arranged curl over his forehead into a limp wisp resembling a lump of seaweed. The Fates are never favorable to the poor wretch. If he does by any chance reach the door in proper condition, she has gone out with her cousin and won't be back till late.

How a young lover made ridiculous by the gawkiness of modern costume must envy the picturesque gallants of seventy years ago! Look at them (on the Christmas cards), with their curly hair and natty hats, their well-shaped legs incased in smalls, their dainty Hessian boots, their ruffling frills, their canes and dangling seals. No wonder the little maiden in the big poke-bonnet and the light-blue sash casts down her eyes and is completely won. Men could win hearts in clothes like that. But what can you expect from baggy trousers and a monkeyjacket?

Clothes have more effect upon us than we imagine. Our deportment depends upon our dress. Make a man get into seedy, worn-out rags, and he will skulk along with his head hanging down, like a man going out to fetch his own supper beer. But deck out the same article in gorgeous raiment and fine linen, and he will strut down the main thoroughfare, swinging his cane and looking at the girls as perky as a bantam cock.

Clothes alter our very nature. A man could not help being fierce and daring with a plume in his bonnet, a dagger in his belt, and a lot of puffy white things all down his sleeves. But in an ulster he wants to get behind a lamp-post and call police.

I am quite ready to admit that you can find sterling merit, honest worth, deep affection, and all such like virtues of the roast-beef-and-plum-pudding school as much, and perhaps more, under broadcloth and tweed as ever existed beneath silk and velvet; but the spirit of that knightly chivalry that "rode a tilt for lady's love" and "fought for lady's smiles" needs the clatter of steel and the rustle of plumes to summon it from its grave between the dusty folds of tapestry and underneath the musty leaves of moldering chronicles.

The world must be getting old, I think; it dresses so very soberly now. We have been through the infant period of humanity, when we used to run about with nothing on but a long, loose robe, and liked to have our feet bare. And then came the rough, barbaric age, the boyhood of our race. We didn't care what we wore then, but thought it nice to tattoo ourselves all over, and we never did our hair. And after that the world grew into a young man and became foppish. It decked itself in flowing curls and scarlet doublets, and went courting, and bragging, and bouncing—making a brave show.

But all those merry, foolish days of youth are gone, and we are very sober, very solemn—and very stupid, some say—now. The world is a grave, middle-aged gentleman in this nineteenth century, and would be shocked to see itself with a bit of finery on. So it dresses in black coats and trousers, and black hats, and black boots, and, dear me, it is such a very respectable gentleman—to think it could ever have gone gadding about as a troubadour or a knight-errant, dressed in all those fancy colors! Ah, well! we are more sensible in this age.

Or at least we think ourselves so. It is a general theory nowadays that sense and dullness go together.

Goodness is another quality that always goes with blackness. Very good people indeed, you will notice, dress altogether in black, even to gloves and neckties, and they will probably take to black shirts before long. Medium goods indulge in light trousers on week-days, and some of them even go so far as to wear fancy waistcoats. On the other hand, people who care nothing for a future state go about in light suits; and there have been known wretches so abandoned as to wear a white hat. Such people, however, are never spoken of in genteel society, and perhaps I ought not to have referred to them here.

By the way, talking of light suits, have you ever noticed how people stare at you the first time you go out in a new light suit They do not notice it so much afterward. The population of London have got accustomed to it by the third time you wear it. I say "you," because I am not speaking from my own experience. I do not wear such things at all myself. As I said, only sinful people do so.

I wish, though, it were not so, and that one could be good, and respectable, and sensible without making one's self a guy. I look in the glass sometimes at my two long, cylindrical bags (so picturesquely rugged about the knees), my stand-up collar and billycock hat, and wonder what right I have to go about making God's world hideous. Then wild and wicked thoughts come into my heart. I don't want to be good and respectable. (I never can be sensible, I'm told; so that don't matter.) I want to put on lavender-colored tights, with red velvet breeches and a green doublet slashed with yellow; to have a light-blue silk cloak on my shoulder, and a black eagle's plume waving from my hat, and a big sword, and a falcon, and a lance, and a prancing horse, so that I might go about and gladden the eyes of the people. Why should we all try to look like ants crawling over a dust-heap? Why shouldn't we dress a little gayly? I am sure if we did we should be happier.

True, it is a little thing, but we are a little race, and what is the use of our pretending otherwise and spoiling fun? Let philosophers get themselves up like old crows if they like. But let me be a butterfly.

Women, at all events, ought to dress prettily. It is their duty. They are the flowers of the earth and were meant to show it up. We abuse them a good deal, we men; but, goodness knows, the old world would be dull enough without their dresses and fair faces. How they brighten up every place they come into! What a sunny commotion they—relations, of course—-make in our dingy bachelor chambers! and what a delightful litter their ribbons and laces, and gloves and hats, and parasols and 'kerchiefs make! It is as if a wandering rainbow had dropped in to pay us a visit.

It is one of the chief charms of the summer, to my mind, the way our little maids come out in pretty colors. I like to see the pink and blue and white glancing between the trees, dotting the green fields, and flashing back the sunlight. You can see the bright colors such a long way off. There are four white dresses climbing a hill in front of my window now. I can see them distinctly, though it is three miles away. I thought at first they were mile-stones out for a lark. It's so nice to be able to see the darlings a long way off. Especially if they happen to be your wife and your mother-in-law.

Talking of fields and mile-stones reminds me that I want to say, in all seriousness, a few words about women's boots. The women of these islands all wear boots too big for them. They can never get a boot to fit. The bootmakers do not keep sizes small enough.

Over and over again have I known women sit down on the top rail of a stile and declare they could not go a step further because their boots hurt them so; and it has always been the same complaint—too big.

It is time this state of things was altered. In the name of the husbands and fathers of England, I call upon the bootmakers to reform. Our wives, our daughters, and our cousins are not to be lamed and tortured with impunity. Why cannot "narrow twos" be kept more in stock? That is the size I find most women take.

The waist-band is another item of feminine apparel that is always too big. The dressmakers make these things so loose that the hooks and eyes by which they are fastened burst off, every now and then, with a report like thunder.

Why women suffer these wrongs—why they do not insist in having their clothes made small enough for them I cannot conceive. It can hardly be that they are disinclined to trouble themselves about matters of mere dress, for dress is the one subject that they really do think about. It is the only topic they ever get thoroughly interested in, and they talk about it all day long. If you see two women together, you may bet your bottom dollar they are discussing their own or their friends' clothes. You notice a couple of child-like beings conversing by a window, and you wonder what sweet, helpful words are falling from their sainted lips. So you move nearer and then you hear one say:

"So I took in the waist-band and let out a seam, and it fits beautifully now."

"Well," says the other, "I shall wear my plum-colored body to the Jones', with a yellow plastron; and they've got some lovely gloves at Puttick's, only one and eleven pence."

I went for a drive through a part of Derbyshire once with a couple of ladies. It was a beautiful bit of country, and they enjoyed themselves immensely. They talked dressmaking the whole time.

"Pretty view, that," I would say, waving my umbrella round. "Look at those blue distant hills! That little white speck, nestling in the woods, is Chatsworth, and over there—"

"Yes, very pretty indeed," one would reply. "Well, why not get a yard of sarsenet?"

"What, and leave the skirt exactly as it is?"

"Certainly. What place d'ye call this?"

Then I would draw their attention to the fresh beauties that kept sweeping into view, and they would glance round and say "charming," "sweetly pretty," and immediately go off into raptures over each other's pocket-handkerchiefs, and mourn with one another over the decadence of cambric frilling.

I believe if two women were cast together upon a desert island, they would spend each day arguing the respective merits of sea-shells and birds' eggs considered as trimmings, and would have a new fashion in fig-leaves every month.

Very young men think a good deal about clothes, but they don't talk about them to each other. They would not find much encouragement. A fop is not a favorite with his own sex. Indeed, he gets a good deal more abuse from them than is necessary. His is a harmless failing and it soon wears out. Besides, a man who has no foppery at twenty will be a slatternly, dirty-collar, unbrushed-coat man at forty. A little foppishness in a young man is good; it is human. I like to see a young cock ruffle his feathers, stretch his neck, and crow as if the whole world belonged to him. I don't like a modest, retiring man. Nobody does—not really, however much they may prate about modest worth and other things they do not understand.

A meek deportment is a great mistake in the world. Uriah Heap's father was a very poor judge of human nature, or he would not have told his son, as he did, that people liked humbleness. There is nothing annoys them more, as a rule. Rows are half the fun of life, and you can't have rows with humble, meek-answering individuals. They turn away our wrath, and that is just what we do not want. We want to let it out. We have worked ourselves up into a state of exhilarating fury, and then just as we are anticipating the enjoyment of a vigorous set-to, they spoil all our plans with their exasperating humility.

Xantippe's life must have been one long misery, tied to that calmly irritating man, Socrates. Fancy a married woman doomed to live on from day to day without one single quarrel with her husband! A man ought to humor his wife in these things.

Heaven knows their lives are dull enough, poor girls. They have none of the enjoyments we have. They go to no political meetings; they may not even belong to the local amateur parliament; they are excluded from smoking-carriages on the Metropolitan Railway, and they never see a comic paper—or if they do, they do not know it is comic: nobody tells them.

Surely, with existence such a dreary blank for them as this, we might provide a little row for their amusement now and then, even if we do not feel inclined for it ourselves. A really sensible man does so and is loved accordingly, for it is little acts of kindness such as this that go straight to a woman's heart. It is such like proofs of loving self-sacrifice that make her tell her female friends what a good husband he was—after he is dead.

Yes, poor Xantippe must have had a hard time of it. The bucket episode was particularly sad for her. Poor woman! she did think she would rouse him up a bit with that. She had taken the trouble to fill the bucket, perhaps been a long way to get specially dirty water. And she waited for him. And then to be met in such a way, after all! Most likely she sat down and had a good cry afterward. It must have seemed all so hopeless to the poor child; and for all we know she had no mother to whom she could go and abuse him.

What was it to her that her husband was a great philosopher? Great philosophy don't count in married life.

There was a very good little boy once who wanted to go to sea. And the captain asked him what he could do. He said he could do the multiplication-table backward and paste sea-weed in a book; that he knew how many times the word "begat" occurred in the Old Testament; and could recite "The Boy Stood on the Burning Deck" and Wordsworth's "We Are Seven."

"Werry good—werry good, indeed," said the man of the sea, "and ken ye kerry coals?"

It is just the same when you want to marry. Great ability is not required so much as little usefulness. Brains are at a discount in the married state. There is no demand for them, no appreciation even. Our wives sum us up according to a standard of their own, in which brilliancy of intellect obtains no marks. Your lady and mistress is not at all impressed by your cleverness and talent, my dear reader—not in the slightest. Give her a man who can do an errand neatly, without attempting to use his own judgment over it or any nonsense of that kind; and who can be trusted to hold a child the right way up, and not make himself objectionable whenever there is lukewarm mutton for dinner. That is the sort of a husband a sensible woman likes; not one of your scientific or literary nuisances, who go upsetting the whole house and putting everybody out with their foolishness.

On Memory.

"I remember, I remember,
In the days of chill November,
How the blackbird on the—"

I forget the rest. It is the beginning of the first piece of poetry I ever learned; for

"Hey, diddle diddle,
The cat and the fiddle,"

I take no note of, it being of a frivolous character and lacking in the qualities of true poetry. I collected fourpence by the recital of "I remember, I remember." I knew it was fourpence, because they told me that if I kept it until I got twopence more I should have sixpence, which argument, albeit undeniable, moved me not, and the money was squandered, to the best of my recollection, on the very next morning, although upon what memory is a blank.

That is just the way with Memory; nothing that she brings to us is complete. She is a willful child; all her toys are broken. I remember tumbling into a huge dust-hole when a very small boy, but I have not the faintest recollection of ever getting out again; and if memory were all we had to trust to, I should be compelled to believe I was there still.

At another time—some years later—I was assisting at an exceedingly interesting love scene; but the only thing about it I can call to mind distinctly is that at the most critical moment somebody suddenly opened the door and said, "Emily, you're wanted," in a sepulchral tone that gave one the idea the police had come for her. All the tender words she said to me and all the beautiful things I said to her are utterly forgotten.

Life altogether is but a crumbling ruin when we turn to look behind: a shattered column here, where a massive portal stood; the broken shaft of a window to mark my lady's bower; and a moldering heap of blackened stones where the glowing flames once leaped, and over all the tinted lichen and the ivy clinging green.

For everything looms pleasant through the softening haze of time. Even the sadness that is past seems sweet. Our boyish days look very merry to us now, all nutting, hoop, and gingerbread. The snubbings and toothaches and the

Latin verbs are all forgotten—the Latin verbs especially. And we fancy we were very happy when we were hobbledehoys and loved; and we wish that we could love again. We never think of the heartaches, or the sleepless nights, or the hot dryness of our throats, when she said she could never be anything to us but a sister—as if any man wanted more sisters!

Yes, it is the brightness, not the darkness, that we see when we look back. The sunshine casts no shadows on the past. The road that we have traversed stretches very fair behind us. We see not the sharp stones. We dwell but on the roses by the wayside, and the strong briers that stung us are, to our distant eyes, but gentle tendrils waving in the wind. God be thanked that it is so—that the ever-lengthening chain of memory has only pleasant links, and that the bitterness and sorrow of to-day are smiled at on the morrow.

It seems as though the brightest side of everything were also its highest and best, so that as our little lives sink back behind us into the dark sea of forgetfulness, all that which is the lightest and the most gladsome is the last to sink, and stands above the waters, long in sight, when the angry thoughts and smarting pain are buried deep below the waves and trouble us no more.

It is this glamour of the past, I suppose, that makes old folk talk so much nonsense about the days when they were young. The world appears to have been a very superior sort of place then, and things were more like what they ought to be. Boys were boys then, and girls were very different. Also winters were something like winters, and summers not at all the wretched-things we get put off with nowadays. As for the wonderful deeds people did in those times and the extraordinary events that happened, it takes three strong men to believe half of them.

I like to hear one of the old boys telling all about it to a party of youngsters who he knows cannot contradict him. It is odd if, after awhile, he doesn't swear that the moon shone every night when he was a boy, and that tossing mad bulls in a blanket was the favorite sport at his school.

It always has been and always will be the same. The old folk of our grandfathers' young days sang a song bearing exactly the same burden; and the young folk of to-day will drone out precisely similar nonsense for the aggravation of the next generation. "Oh, give me back the good old days of fifty years ago," has been the cry ever since Adam's fifty-first birthday. Take up the literature of 1835, and you will find the poets and novelists asking for the same impossible gift as did the German Minnesingers long before them and the old Norse Saga writers long before that. And for the same thing sighed the early prophets and the philosophers of ancient Greece. From all accounts, the world has been getting worse and worse ever since it was created. All I can say is that it must have been a remarkably delightful place when it was first opened to the public, for it is very pleasant even now if you only keep as much as possible in the sunshine and take the rain good-temperedly.

Yet there is no gainsaying but that it must have been somewhat sweeter in that dewy morning of creation, when it was young and fresh, when the feet of the tramping millions had not trodden its grass to dust, nor the din of the myriad cities chased the silence forever away. Life must have been noble and solemn to those free-footed, loose-robed fathers of the human race, walking hand in hand with God under the great sky. They lived in sunkissed tents amid the lowing herds. They took their simple wants from the loving hand of Nature. They toiled and talked and thought; and the great earth rolled around in stillness, not yet laden with trouble and wrong.

Those days are past now. The quiet childhood of Humanity, spent in the far-off forest glades and by the murmuring rivers, is gone forever; and human life is deepening down to manhood amid tumult, doubt, and hope. Its age of restful peace is past. It has its work to finish and must hasten on. What that work may be—what this world's share is in the great design—we know not, though our unconscious hands are helping to accomplish it. Like the tiny coral insect working deep under the dark waters, we strive and struggle each for our own little ends, nor dream of the vast fabric we are building up for God.

Let us have done with vain regrets and longings for the days that never will be ours again. Our work lies in front, not behind us; and "Forward!" is our motto. Let us not sit with folded hands, gazing upon the past as if it were the building; it is but the foundation. Let us not waste heart and life thinking of what might have been and forgetting the may be that lies before us. Opportunities flit by while we sit regretting the chances we have lost, and the happiness that comes to us we heed not, because of the happiness that is gone.

Years ago, when I used to wander of an evening from the fireside to the pleasant land of fairy-tales, I met a doughty knight and true. Many dangers had he overcome, in many lands had been; and all men knew him for a brave and well-tried knight, and one that knew not fear; except, maybe, upon such seasons when even a brave man might feel afraid and yet not be ashamed. Now, as this knight one day was pricking wearily along a toilsome road, his heart misgave him and was sore within him because of the trouble of the way. Rocks, dark and of a monstrous size, hung high above his head, and like enough it seemed unto the knight that they should fall and he lie low beneath them. Chasms there were on either side, and darksome caves wherein fierce robbers lived, and dragons, very terrible, whose jaws dripped blood. And upon the road there hung a darkness as of night. So it came over that good knight that he would no more press forward, but seek another road, less grievously beset with difficulty unto his gentle steed. But when in haste he turned and looked behind, much marveled our brave knight, for lo! of all the way that he had ridden there was naught for eye to see; but at his horse's heels there yawned a mighty gulf, whereof no man might ever spy the bottom, so deep was that same gulf. Then when Sir Ghelent saw that of going back there was none, he prayed to good Saint Cuthbert, and setting spurs into his steed rode forward bravely and most joyously. And naught harmed him.

There is no returning on the road of life. The frail bridge of time on which we tread sinks back into eternity at every step we take. The past is gone from us forever. It is gathered in and garnered. It belongs to us no more. No single word can ever be unspoken; no single step retraced. Therefore it beseems us as true knights to prick on bravely, not idly weep because we cannot now recall.

A new life begins for us with every second. Let us go forward joyously to meet it. We must press on whether we will or no, and we shall walk better with our eyes before us than with them ever cast behind.

A friend came to me the other day and urged me very eloquently to learn some wonderful system by which you never forgot anything. I don't know why he was so eager on the subject, unless it be that I occasionally borrow an umbrella and have a knack of coming out, in the middle of a game of whist, with a mild "Lor! I've been thinking all along that clubs were trumps." I declined the suggestion, however, in spite of the advantages he so attractively set forth. I have no wish to remember everything. There are many things in most men's lives that had better be forgotten. There is that time, many years ago, when we did not act quite as honorably, quite as uprightly, as we perhaps should have done—that unfortunate deviation from the path of strict probity we once committed, and in which, more unfortunate still, we were found out—that act of folly, of meanness, of wrong. Ah, well! we paid the penalty, suffered the maddening hours of vain remorse, the hot agony of shame, the scorn, perhaps, of those we loved. Let us forget. Oh, Father Time, lift with your kindly hands those bitter memories from off our overburdened hearts, for griefs are ever coming to us with the coming hours, and our little strength is only as the day.

Not that the past should be buried. The music of life would be mute if the chords of memory were snapped asunder. It is but the poisonous weeds, not the flowers, that we should root out from the garden of Mnemosyne. Do you remember Dickens' "Haunted Man"—how he prayed for forgetfulness, and how, when his prayer was answered, he prayed for memory once more? We do not want all the ghosts laid. It is only the haggard, cruel-eyed specters that we flee from. Let the gentle, kindly phantoms haunt us as they will; we are not afraid of them.

Ah me! the world grows very full of ghosts as we grow older. We need not seek in dismal church-yards nor sleep in moated granges to see the shadowy faces and hear the rustling of their garments in the night. Every house, every room, every creaking chair has its own particular ghost. They haunt the empty chambers of our lives, they throng around us like dead leaves whirled in the autumn wind. Some are living, some are dead. We know not. We clasped their hands once, loved them, quarreled with them, laughed with them, told them our thoughts and hopes and aims, as they told us theirs, till it seemed our very hearts had joined in a grip that would defy the puny power of Death. They are gone now; lost to us forever. Their eyes will never look into ours again and their voices we shall never hear. Only their ghosts come to us and talk with us. We see them, dim and shadowy, through our tears. We stretch our yearning hands to them, but they are air.

Ghosts! They are with us night and day. They walk beside us in the busy street under the glare of the sun. They sit by us in the twilight at home. We see their little faces looking from the windows of the old school-house. We meet them in the woods and lanes where we shouted and played as boys. Hark! cannot you hear their low laughter from behind the blackberry-bushes and their distant whoops along the grassy glades? Down here, through the quiet fields and by the wood, where the evening shadows are lurking, winds the path where we used to watch for her at sunset. Look, she is there now, in the dainty white frock we knew so well, with the big bonnet dangling from her little hands and the sunny brown hair all tangled. Five thousand miles away! Dead for all we know! What of that? She is beside us now, and we can look into her laughing eyes and hear her voice. She will vanish at the stile by the wood and we shall be alone; and the shadows will creep out across the fields and the night wind will sweep past moaning. Ghosts! they are always with us and always will be while the sad old world keeps echoing to the sob of long good-bys, while the cruel ships sail away across the great seas, and the cold green earth lies heavy on the hearts of those we loved.

But, oh, ghosts, the world would be sadder still without you. Come to us and speak to us, oh you ghosts of our old loves! Ghosts of playmates, and of sweethearts, and old friends, of all you laughing boys and girls, oh, come to us and be with us, for the world is very lonely, and new friends and faces are not like the old, and we cannot love them, nay, nor laugh with them as we have loved and laughed with you. And when we walked together, oh, ghosts of our youth, the world was very gay and bright; but now it has grown old and we are growing weary, and only you can bring the brightness and the freshness back to us.

Memory is a rare ghost-raiser. Like a haunted house, its walls are ever echoing to unseen feet. Through the broken casements we watch the flitting shadows of the dead, and the saddest shadows of them all are the shadows of our own dead selves.

Oh, those young bright faces, so full of truth and honor, of pure, good thoughts, of noble longings, how reproachfully they look upon us with their deep, clear eyes!

I fear they have good cause for their sorrow, poor lads. Lies and cunning and disbelief have crept into our hearts since those preshaving days—and we meant to be so great and good.

It is well we cannot see into the future. There are few boys of fourteen who would not feel ashamed of themselves at forty.

I like to sit and have a talk sometimes with that odd little chap that was myself long ago. I think he likes it too, for he comes so often of an evening when I am alone with my pipe, listening to the whispering of the flames. I see his solemn little face looking at me through the scented smoke as it floats upward, and I smile at him; and he smiles back at me, but his is such a grave, old-fashioned smile. We chat about old times; and now and then he takes me by the hand, and then we slip through the black bars of the grate and down the dusky glowing caves to the land that lies behind the firelight. There we find the days that used to be, and we wander along them together. He tells me as we walk all he thinks and feels. I laugh at him now and then, but the next moment I wish I had not, for he looks so grave I am ashamed of being frivolous. Besides, it is not showing proper respect to one so much older than myself—to one who was myself so very long before I became myself.

We don't talk much at first, but look at one another; I down at his curly hair and little blue bow, he up sideways at me as he trots. And some-how I fancy the shy, round eyes do not altogether approve of me, and he heaves a little sigh, as though he were disappointed. But after awhile his bashfulness wears off and he begins to chat. He tells me his favorite fairy-tales, he can do up to six times, and he has a guinea-pig, and pa says fairy-tales ain't true; and isn't it a pity? 'cos he would so like to be a knight and fight a dragon and marry a beautiful princess. But he takes a more practical view of life when he reaches seven, and would prefer to grow up be a bargee, and earn a lot of money. Maybe this is the consequence of falling in love, which he does about this time with the young lady at the milk shop aet. six. (God bless her little ever-dancing feet, whatever size they may be now!) He must be very fond of her, for he gives her one day his chiefest treasure, to wit, a huge pocket-knife with four rusty blades and a corkscrew, which latter has a knack of working itself out in some mysterious manner and sticking into its owner's leg. She is an affectionate little thing, and she throws her arms round his neck and kisses him for it, then and there, outside the shop. But the stupid world (in the person of the boy at the cigar emporium next door) jeers at such tokens of love. Whereupon my young friend very properly prepares to punch the head of the boy at the cigar emporium next door; but fails in the attempt, the boy at the cigar emporium next door punching his instead.

And then comes school life, with its bitter little sorrows and its joyous shoutings, its jolly larks, and its hot tears falling on beastly Latin grammars and silly old copy-books. It is at school that he injures himself for life—as I firmly believe—trying to pronounce German; and it is there, too, that he learns of the importance attached by the French nation to pens, ink, and paper. "Have you pens, ink, and paper?" is the first question asked by one Frenchman of another on their meeting. The other fellow has not any of them, as a rule, but says that the uncle of his brother has got them all three. The first fellow doesn't appear to care a hang about the uncle of the other fellow's brother; what he wants to know now is, has the neighbor of the other fellow's mother got 'em? "The neighbor of my mother has no pens, no ink, and no paper," replies the other man, beginning to get wild. "Has the child of thy female gardener some pens, some ink, or some paper?" He has him there. After worrying enough about these wretched inks, pens, and paper to make everybody miserable, it turns out that the child of his own female gardener hasn't any. Such a discovery would shut up any one but a French exercise man. It has no effect at all, though, on this shameless creature. He never thinks of apologizing, but says his aunt has some mustard.

So in the acquisition of more or less useless knowledge, soon happily to be forgotten, boyhood passes away. The red-brick school-house fades from view, and we turn down into the world's high-road. My little friend is no longer little now. The short jacket has sprouted tails. The battered cap, so useful as a combination of pocket-handkerchief, drinking-cup, and weapon of attack, has grown high and glossy; and instead of a slate-pencil in his mouth there is a cigarette, the smoke of which troubles him, for it will get up his nose. He tries a cigar a little later on as being more stylish—a big black Havanna. It doesn't seem altogether to agree with him, for I find him sitting over a bucket in the back kitchen afterward, solemnly swearing never to smoke again.

And now his mustache begins to be almost visible to the naked eye, whereupon he immediately takes to brandy-and-sodas and fancies himself a man. He talks about "two to one against the favorite," refers to actresses as

"Little Emmy" and "Kate" and "Baby," and murmurs about his "losses at cards the other night" in a style implying that thousands have been squandered, though, to do him justice, the actual amount is most probably one-and-twopence. Also, if I see aright—for it is always twilight in this land of memories—he sticks an eyeglass in his eye and stumbles over everything.

His female relations, much troubled at these things, pray for him (bless their gentle hearts!) and see visions of Old Bailey trials and halters as the only possible outcome of such reckless dissipation; and the prediction of his first school-master, that he would come to a bad end, assumes the proportions of inspired prophecy.

He has a lordly contempt at this age for the other sex, a blatantly good opinion of himself, and a sociably patronizing manner toward all the elderly male friends of the family. Altogether, it must be confessed, he is somewhat of a nuisance about this time.

It does not last long, though. He falls in love in a little while, and that soon takes the bounce out of him. I notice his boots are much too small for him now, and his hair is fearfully and wonderfully arranged. He reads poetry more than he used, and he keeps a rhyming dictionary in his bedroom. Every morning Emily Jane finds scraps of torn-up paper on the floor and reads thereon of "cruel hearts and love's deep darts," of "beauteous eyes and lovers' sighs," and much more of the old, old song that lads so love to sing and lassies love to listen to while giving their dainty heads a toss and pretending never to hear.

The course of love, however, seems not to have run smoothly, for later on he takes more walking exercise and less sleep, poor boy, than is good for him; and his face is suggestive of anything but wedding-bells and happiness ever after.

And here he seems to vanish. The little, boyish self that has grown up beside me as we walked is gone.

I am alone and the road is very dark. I stumble on, I know not how nor care, for the way seems leading nowhere, and there is no light to guide.

But at last the morning comes, and I find that I have grown into myself.
THE END.

Made in the USA
San Bernardino, CA
08 June 2015